C000138646

Ben Braddock

LUVVIE

or
Live Fast,
Die Young

The beginning of this story
actually happened though not to
me.

Some of what follows is also true.

"LUVVIE" is a humorous term for an actor.
(Oxford English Dictionary)

Contents

Part One

Chapter One
By the time…

By the time you read this I may or may not be dead…

Chapter Two
Buy the time...

You're still reading?

Good. But please don't expect F Scott Fitzgerald or Steinbeck or Hemingway from the get go. I'm new to this novel writing game. Nobody promised you this would be the next great American novel. I'm not even American for starters.

Our first step on this particular journey takes place on the eve of my fortieth birthday and included among those present are one member of my family, such as it is, and a few friends, such as they are, some close, some who simply had nothing better to do that evening. As we go along you'll get to know some of them a little better but I expect what you want to know right now is why I can't be confident that I'll survive until the end of the story.

As far as your favourite writers go, I'm guessing Dickens isn't your thing but, for all I know, you might want the story to build slowly with detailed character descriptions and all that kind of guff. And, if I were a more traditional story teller who'd won numerous fancy writing awards in the past for style and general dullness, I might do that. But I'm really not expecting a Pulitzer prize for fiction from this and nor should you.

I'm not going to start this book like that for two reasons. First, I don't like that sort of book and second it was a really rubbish party and the less said about it the better. One of the reasons I thought it was a rubbish party is that I don't like parties, especially birthday parties, reserving a particular dislike for parties which coincide with *my* birthday.

My friends and family know this, so, well… why bother? Why go to any trouble for someone who hates parties and particularly hates their own birthday parties. We'll get back to my friends and family later. Who was there and why they were there and who wasn't there and why not later. A lot of the people who were at that party aren't really important to the story so… why bother?

And why bother going to any trouble like hiring a stripper, a traditional way of celebrating a single man's fortieth year? Presumably it signifies that it's all downhill from here and that gravity, contrary to what you learned in school, is not a constant force and acts with increasing vigour on the body in a downward direction with every year past forty.

But my friends hadn't booked a stripper. They'd hired an amateur psychic and magician of dubious skill, whose idea of fun or supplementing his income was to turn up at appalling social gatherings and make them worse. He was such a dreadful magician that it was something of a relief when he swapped playing cards for tarot cards and proceeded to tell my fortune. Most of which was nonsense. You have not yet met the love of your life… that sort of thing. Well, any fool could have told you that. If I had met the love of my life it stands to reason she might have come to my party.

The Great Alfonso's last two predictions were somewhat more tantalising.

"You will win a prize in the next lottery."

"You've put your cards on the table there," I said.

"The next lottery draw is in about ten minutes. How much am I going to win? Enough to hire a stripper?"

"Enough to change your life."

"Gosh, as much as that… How much is that by the way?"

"That may depend on your next and final card" he replied with as much psychic grandeur as he could muster.

"Go on then. The clock's ticking," I said.

The psychic began to turn over the next tarot card…

He stopped and replaced it on top of the pack.

"Never mind… That's the end of your reading".

"You can't stop now. Come on, I can take it. Between you and me I don't really believe in psychics."

"Very well. If you're sure."

"Quite sure."

The psychic again turned over the next tarot card…

DEATH… The Death Card….

If there had been any party spirit still bubbling at that moment that's the sort of thing which might have put a damper on it. But this party was so… well… dead that the appearance of the Death Card actually livened things up a bit. Or at least it did for my best friend, Stuart, who was the first to greet the news with a snicker. The first but not the only one and within a few seconds the prediction of my imminent death filled the room with happy laughter that had been notably absent hitherto. Charming, no?

'Sorry, I usually take that card out of the pack for parties..."

"Why? Afraid you'll spoil the mood?" I asked.

"It hasn't spoiled my mood," said Stuart.

"I should explain that the card doesn't necessarily spell death, you know," the psychic continued.

"So, good news, then?"

"Shut up, Stuart. Let the man finish."

"As the actress said to the bishop."

"Shut up, will you?"

"Okey dokey. Let's hear what the Great Alfonso has to say."

The psychic drew breath and continued, apparently immune to any inference of sarcasm which, for all I know, may be a common failing among incompetent magicians and psychics. It was certainly not one likely to promise a lasting friendship with Stuart.

"The Death Card often implies a change in life. An abrupt change."

"Unless it's the other thing..."

"Thank you, Stuart. We're trying to move on from there."

"The change is usually complete and often unexpected and unpleasant," the Great Alfonso continued unhelpfully as if auditioning to be Stuart's straight man.

"A bit like death then," Stuart said.

Either the Great Alfonso was starting to catch on to Stuart's sense of humour or else his allotted, or failing that paid for, time was up. He stood up.

"And when will my time be up?" I asked. "When will this final, unexpected...?"

"And unpleasant..."

"Thank you, Stuart... When will this big change..."

"Or death..."

"Happen?"

I gave Stuart my best Paddington stare and this silenced him for now. Either that or he'd just run out of material.

"I can't say exactly but since the prediction may be linked to your birthday..."

"Which is tomorrow. Or in about five hour's time to be exact."

"Yes, I can't be exactly sure but if you make it through tomorrow you've probably got a year. If it's not this birthday, I'd say it will very likely happen on or around your next birthday."

"Very comforting."

"Or anytime between now and then."

"Super, thanks so much for coming. Can you find your own way out?"

The Great Alfonso gathered his cards together with an apologetic smile.

"Happy Birthday on the morrow by the way. Hope it all goes well. I expect you're used to surprises, you being an April Fool" he said, replacing the tarot cards in their box.

"So that prediction was what, a joke? A prank?" I asked

"Sadly, no. Sorry."

"Well, thanks. I've always hated my birthday but you've made this one really special. Very memorable indeed."

"Best one yet," Stuart said, palming a fiver by way of a tip as he shook hands warmly with the Great Alfonso, who bade farewell with an elaborate bow and made for the door.

"Well, that livened things up no end" I said after he'd gone.

"Pun intended?" asked Stuart.

And strangely enough the psychic's prediction of my impending doom or at the very least impending unpleasantness did further liven up proceedings and the party continued with a bit more fizz for a good five minutes before some bright spark turned on the television so we could hear the results of the draw for the lottery.

****

"Bloody hell!" I said, looking at my ticket... Then back at the television.

"Bloody hell!" I said looking from the television back down to my ticket.

"How much did you win?"

I didn't see who asked the question. I didn't see anything other than the letters and numbers and the matching sequence on the television.

"Enough to be cryogenically frozen, I think….
Should the need arise."

" So… enough to buy yourself some time… Should
the need arise." I looked up at Stuart and attempted
something that I hoped approximated to a smile.

Chapter Three

Life's a Lottery…

I've never really mastered the art of smiling. Laughter comes easily enough if I hear something genuinely funny, but laughter's an instinctive thing, like cursing when you stub your toe. Perhaps smiling is as instinctive as laughter if you're one of the shiny, happy people REM used to sing about, but I'm not one of those people and, now I think about it, I never saw Michael Stipe smile much either. Even when he was singing about shiny, happy folk.

Smiling for photos is about as much fun for me as a ticklish kiss from an ageing aunt, which never endeared me to my agent (or to my aunt) when I was a struggling actor in London and boxes of 10 x 8 photos bearing my pained grimace remained stacked in her office as a reminder of my dormant career as actor, a monument to just one of my dormant careers. And, by dormant, I mean failed.

I'm a bit of a Renaissance Man, you see. I've failed in any number of different careers. Perhaps that's why I've never mastered the happy, natural smile of those blessed with perfect pearly whites and straightforward lives. In any case I'm left to conclude that, while others can control what their face is expressing, it's never been an area of excellence for me.

So I don't know exactly what my facial expression conveyed at the precise moment of my lottery win. Let's go with surprise.

And I don't know if winning a million pounds on the lottery would be a life changing event for everyone, but it certainly changed mine for the next few minutes. I hadn't won the *actual* lottery. I'd won the millionaire raffle. Four letters denoting one of twelve colours like BLUE and GOLD and AQUA followed by an eight digit number. I didn't even know that aqua was a colour. I thought it was the Latin for 'water' or the name of the girl who sang *I'm a Barbie Girl,* but there it was, printed on the little pink slip, followed by those eight life changing digits.

The unexpected news that their host was now a millionaire changed the tone of the party suddenly and completely. For the next five minutes it was a bit like New Year's except that for once I was the recipient of most of the kisses. More kisses than I'd had in a whole year of New Years if such a thing were possible.

"It appears money can buy you happiness," I announced raising my glass by way of a toast.

"Or failing that a number of attentive women," said Stuart.

"Right now I'm going to call that a distinction without a difference."

"You can afford your own stripper now."

"Yes, but can it buy me more time?"

"You're not still harping on about that Death Card, are you?"

"It makes you stop and think. A big change, the guy said. A life changing moment."

"Or the other thing… Death."

"But either way, painful."

"You'll probably see quite a lot more of me. I've never had a rich friend before."

"That will no doubt be painful, of course, but it's not what you'd call an abrupt change. I see a fair amount of you already. Especially when you're broke."

"So very little change there. Speaking of which, you can't see your way to reimbursing me for that fiver I gave him, can you?"

"And so it begins," I said handing over a five pound note.

"So what's the plan, lottery man?"

"I haven't the slightest idea. Normally all I have to worry about is what I'm going to do tomorrow. Which pair of slightly elderly, saggy trousers should I wear?"

"If it helps you can give all the money to me. You could be the saggy *Ragged Trousered Philanthropist.*"

In between acting jobs, which were as thin on the ground for Stuart as for me, he often worked in a second hand bookshop for a friend for whom the business was little more than hobby. Or a way to spend time away from her appalling husband. Quite possibly both. Unfortunately this only fuelled Stuart's enthusiasm for jokes of a literary nature.

"Did you know the original title page of that book carried the warning, "the story of twelve months in Hell, told by one of the damned."

"Remind me to read it. It might help me plan what to do with the next year."

"Assuming you've got that long."

"You're not going to let this lie, are you?"

"Not as long as it's funny."

"It stopped being funny some time ago."

"Cheer up, you've just won the lottery."

"But for how long? How long have I got? It's not very nice living under a possible sentence of death. Assuming it's true. And if it's not true-"

"It's not true. We got the Great Alfonso off the internet. Not exactly a guarantee of competence or truth. And whether it's true or not shouldn't make any difference to how you live your life. I know what you should do with your next year. *Carpe Diem.*"

"Learn Latin? I didn't like it much the first time around."

"Live every day as if it were going to be your last; for one day you're sure to be right."

"*Breaker Morant*. Good movie and strangely appropriate. He was about to face a firing squad. You're really very wise in your own way, so long as you're quoting books or movies."

"Every man dies. Not every man really lives."

"*Braveheart*. Okay, you can stop now. I think I get your point. Subtlety never being one of your stronger suits."

"Buy a new suit. That would be a start. Dump the saggy trousers. Clothes maketh the man."

"Where does that one come from?"

"I think that one may be mine. I might have made that one up or paraphrased a bit. No, hold on, it's coming… *Hamlet*- 'Costly thy habit as thy purse can buy… but not expressed in fancy; rich, not gaudy; for the apparel oft proclaims the man."

"You forgot something. 'Give every man thine ear, but few thy voice'."

"I've got that one on a coffee mug," Stuart said.

"I know. I've made you coffee in it. The irony never escapes me."

"Meow. Saucer of milk for the cat who just won the lottery?"

"I think I'm tired of playing Hamlet hockey. His life expectancy wasn't that great."

"You could give your acting career another go. You could just about buy your own small theatre now. Turn it into a barn."

"I was never really cut out to be the lead. Just another spear carrier, that's me."

"What you need is a good old fashioned mid-life crisis. To be honest, you needed one before but now you can actually afford one."

"You mean buy a little red sports car and start dating a gold digger."

"Let's start with the sports car. Baby steps…Hi, Fiona, have I told you you look incredibly sexy tonight?"

"Not lately, Stuart. It's nearly midnight. Can I be the first to give the Birthday Boy a kiss?"

Fiona kissed me on the cheek and gave me a hug that I wished could last forever, or failing that, a little longer. She smelled faintly of vanilla. All too soon the hug and the hint of vanilla were in the past. Like the remotest chance that Fiona and I would ever be a thing.

"Well, Birthday Boy. How are you going to spend all that lovely money?"

"Don't you start."

"I like Stuart's idea of buying a sports car. I look sensational with the top down," she said, eyes twinkling and flashing the sort of smile only people with perfect teeth whose eyes can twinkle can smile.

"I bet you say that to all the boys…"

"Only the ones who've just won the lottery, Stuart. Be a dear and get me another drink."

My hopes of a long and meaningful conversation with Fiona were regrettably short-lived and imaginings of what Fiona might look like, top down, all too fleeting and mostly in the distant past. Before Stuart could come back with a drink she announced that she had to be up early in the morning and with another kiss on the cheek she was gone, moving through the assembled gathering of minor characters and spear carriers with the grace of a former ballet dancer. Which is what she was. Had been once. Until she got too tall. And long, legged, lovely…

And way out of my league, lottery win or not.

Chapter Four

Shopping and F***king

Fans of the London theatre scene of a certain age might remember Mark Ravenhill's f**cking stage play of that name, produced at the Royal Court Theatre by a company called *Out of Joint*. Out of joint was mostly how I felt around that time because it was the sort of show I never got auditions for as an actor and got the sort of plaudits and attention that no play of mine ever did as a writer.

Yes, that's right I was briefly a struggling, and for struggling, read failed, playwright as well as an actor back in the day I shared a flat in Stockwell on a street whose only claim to fame was that it had been home to one of the victims of the Stockwell Strangler a few years before. I shared the flat with Stuart. Two struggling (failing) actors together. Probably not a healthy combination.

Believe it or not Stuart made more money selling second hand books, none of which included my plays which, unlike "Shopping and F**cking", were never published except in obscure anthologies with titles like *Audition Scenes for Actors*, read only by other struggling, failing actors like myself. Don't bother looking for them. They probably all had very short print runs and are therefore extremely hard to find. You won't even find them in a second hand book store. The only place you're likely to find them is on my bookshelves. One of the courtesy copies sent to me by the publishers instead of.. oh, I don't know… paying me? Regrettably their rarity has never added to their value.

Unlike any of the characters in Ravenhill's play, shopping was never one of my favourite activities for some reason (see above, to actor/writer failed, add the word starving) and as for fucking? Forget it. Not never but not often either. I certainly never associated shopping with fucking or any other pleasant activity because, unlike one of the characters in Mark Ravenhill's play, I have never had oral sex in Harvey Nichols.

I imagine if I tried anything like that I'd get caught, possibly arrested, or at the very least receive a polite request not to darken the doors of Harvey Nicks again. Or possibly the request might be less than polite if I were still looking poor and wearing saggy breeks. That's slang for trousers by the way if unlike me you're not from north of the border. Perhaps we'll cover my early life, a Scottish childhood, later. Or not.

I was still not suitably dressed for a shopping trip to the West End like the recent lottery winner I was, having not as yet collected the cheque. I had, however, telephoned the good people at the lottery and found myself the beneficiary of a seemingly enormous line of credit. Taking all this into account I decided to go shopping online.

And quickly tiring of shopping for trousers- I don't know about you but nothing I've ever bought online fits, hence trousers that are saggy- I decided to follow Stuart's advice.

I bought a little red sports car...

But you don't want to hear about shopping. If you wanted to read about that sort of thing you'd read *Bridget Jones' Diary* again or perhaps you've never read *Bridget Jones' Diary* but want to read more about f**king...

In that case I can only suggest you read Mark Ravenhill's play, available in all good book stores. Or try the internet. It's full of that sort of thing though none of it bears any likeness to my experience of horizontal jogging up to that point. They seem to do it very fast and for a very long time.

My recent encounters with that sort of activity in real life were anything but recent. One of them included a brief fling with a girl who carried me into her bedroom over her shoulder in a fireman's lift and warned me on our first night together that her cherry red bed head made her look like Sideshow Bob the next day. It did. A valediction, forbidding morning, to misquote John Donne. And yes, I was a little scared when I opened my eyes in the cold light of dawn.

Busy old fool, unruly Sun,
Why dost thou thus,
Through windows and through curtains call on us?

22

"Hello, Bob…"

With apologies, once more, to John Donne for ruining his poem. But seriously, it really was like waking up next to Sideshow Bob.

My most recent encounter of all was after a drunken party on a barge on the Thames. Just as I was falling asleep on a tiny bunk a girl from New Zealand, known only to me as Kiwi, climbed into my sleeping bag beside me to "share my warmth". This pleasant and entirely unexpected surprise led to a few minutes of mutual fumbling and rummaging in the dark before she left as abruptly and unexpectedly as she had arrived.

She took me to one side the next morning and explained herself with the not altogether flattering line,

"I'm sorry. I thought you were someone else."

Chapter Five

Here's to you, Mrs Robinson

When you buy a little red sports car off the internet, it comes in a crate. Who knew?

Not me. This was like every birthday and Christmas (not keen on them either) rolled into one only this time I'd got something I actually wanted. Actually *always* wanted.

For the first time in my life I wasn't disappointed when I unwrapped a parcel or rather when I jemmied open the wooden crate with a crowbar (£14.99 on eBay for a 5 piece set of varying degrees of brute force) to get at my dream car, a 1966 Alfa Romeo Spider Duetto.

That's right, all you petrol heads, the very same little red sports car driven by Dustin Hoffman in *The Graduate.* Not the actual car. I'm guessing that might cost all of my lottery winnings and more, but one just like it and still pretty pricey for a car that probably won't start in the rain but hey- it's Italian and it's red and it's all mine.

My dream car.

I'm not a petrol head myself but I'd grown up loving the movie and wanting that car since my dad took me to see the film. No idea why he took me to see that particular film when it finally reached our local cinema about fifteen years after its first release. Maybe he'd seen it before. I don't remember.

My dad was one of the good guys, the sort of small town doctor you don't find any more. A dinner time teller of tales that wandered by way of tangents and digressions to a fondly remembered familiar conclusion. For good or ill I've inherited some of his character, mostly for good I hope. But taking me to see *The Graduate?* My dad was so square that he made Benjamin Braddock's parents look hip. Perhaps he took me because he was a bit of a petrol head himself, though he would never have heard of that term. He was a guy who just liked cars, I suppose, with a particular liking for the Citroen DS series, the only car I know that has its back wheels closer together than its friends at the front, and whose innovative but floaty suspension meant that, when I was a child, any journey longer than an hour required frequent pit stops so that I could throw up at the side of the road. Which I didn't love and to this day I can't see a picture of a Citroen DS without feeling a little queazy.

But I loved my new little, red sports car just like I loved *The Graduate*. That's why I'm called Ben Braddock, after the Dustin Hoffman character. Not my real name you understand. That's my stage name and the name I used to write under. My real name is so dull and ordinary that someone else in the actors' union already had it, which is why I had to change it.

You can't be a member of the union with the same name as another actor. It's so that if they want to want to cast Brad Pitt or Robert Redford in a movie the guy who shows up for the meeting is indeed Brad Pitt or Robert Redford and not, well, someone like me. Actually, I don't think Bob auditions any more. Probably hasn't for quite some time. Once you're famous you don't have to put up with all the crap that struggling actors do. You don't do theatre above a pub or something called "profit share", where there's never any profit, in the forlorn hope that this might lead to your big break.

And you don't have to share a dressing room with fifteen other actors, male and female, fighting for mirror space. You get one to yourself and if you're Ethel Merman, for all I know, on your dressing room they really have "hung a star".

On a film set you've got your own trailer with a fruit basket and an assistant to Mr Redford who's probably a struggling actor who hates you because you're famous and have your own trailer with a fruit basket and all your struggling actor assistant gets out of it is long hours and a mention somewhere near the bottom of the credits.

Or did he just retire?

I think he did.

Way back when Robert Redford was still only quite famous, he did in fact audition for *The Graduate* before they gave it to Hoffman. And thank goodness they did. Can you imagine the implausibility of Redford graduating from college in the Sixties and still being a virgin? There's a story that the director had to explain to Redford why he wasn't right for the role. He did this by asking the actor if he'd ever "struck out" with a girl. Now Redford went to college on a baseball scholarship so he knew what "struck out" meant, but not when it came to girls. So he asked the director-

"What do you mean, struck out?"

To which the director replied-

"Exactly."

Now I'd long ago struck out with Fiona or, to be more exact, I never went to bat. Never had the nerve, the confidence, the inches… In height, in height. Don't be smutty. I'm five foot seven and she's, I don't know, five foot more. Too tall to be a ballet dancer back in a time when ballerinas were all tiny. Certainly not closing on six feet and towering over their male partner, making it not so much pas de deus as pas de dwarf.

I'd met Fiona when I was rehearsing a musical that was less Sondheim, more Springtime for Hitler. Fiona had long since given up performing to run her own dance school for kids. That's right, folks. There's money to be made in teaching little girls how to point their toe. Who knew?

Who knew? She knew.

She'd come in to rehearsals as a favour to the director who was a friend of a friend to help us stamp our feet at approximately the same time.

According to legend when Fred Astaire did his first screen test the initial verdict was "can't sing. Can't act. Can dance a little." Which just goes to show that some people can make an arse of themselves most of the time. And if you're an actor your career can hang by a thread and an idiot is holding the scissors.

If you're not convinced, the initial verdict on Clark Gable's first screen test was "ears too big. He'll never make it in this business". Since Gable went on to be the highest paid actor in Hollywood… You get my point whatever that was. Either "don't put your daughter on the stage, Mrs Worthington" or never give up on your dream. You pays your money and you makes your choice.

Can dance a little was about the best any of us in that cast could manage. Not so much Fred and Ginger, more like Dr. F's monster putting on his top hat and hoofing it in *Young Frankenstein*. I'd like to say I showed the natural grace of a Baryshnikov… I'd like to say that but… I certainly wasn't the worst.

One older actor who in appearance did slightly resemble Clive Dunn showed the same flair for moving his feet in time with everyone else as Corporal Jones in *Dad's Army*. If nothing else I was an extremely attentive pupil. Don't get me wrong, I'm not some kind of pervy type. At least I try very hard not to be or, if all else fails, I try hard not to to stare. But let's just say heads turned when Fiona first walked into the church hall where we were rehearsing. Some people look good in lycra, some do not. That's the way it crumbles, cookie-wise.

Through having some of the same friends who were mutually friends of friends, Fiona and I had stayed in touch without at first being pals until eventually I became her semi-regular companion to parties and gallery openings on the beautiful people circuit during the times she was briefly single or fighting with whichever boyfriend was currently jerk of the month. This happened surprisingly often since Fiona seemed either to attract total jerks or to be attracted to them. The jury was still out on that one. Either way, she was certainly cat nip to any stray tom so long as he was tall, handsome, and incapable of remaining faithful.

Maybe it comes with the territory of being male, handsome, and horny that, like Robert Redford, you've never struck out with a girl and this leads you to believe you can behave like an arsehole because, if you piss off one girlfriend, there'll be another one along in a minute.

So to cut to the chase and Fiona was always more chased than chaste, I received not altogether infrequent invitations to accompany her to various functions which at least gave me access to champagne and nibbles of varying degrees of yumminess (caviar revolting, oysters… one is enough). And these invitations were sufficiently frequent for me to acquire a tolerance, if not a liking, for oysters and a reason to keep at least one pair of trousers that weren't too saggy.

In short we became pals. I was her best male friend and she my best girl friend. I became her principal shoulder to cry on after each and every break up. It turns out I can be a pretty good listener for a bloke and she had surprisingly few female friends. Or perhaps that wasn't so surprising.

Only those in rock solid relationships were likely to want someone like Fiona around, which was probably a little unfair, since to my certain knowledge, she'd never stolen anyone's boyfriend. She didn't need to. And in a strange way I actually enjoyed her break-up tears. I guess sometimes it's just nice to be needed and now there was only ever the trace of a lingering regret that on those occasions there was never any chance of Harry shagging Sally. We were irretrievably in the "friends' zone" as they say in American sitcoms and yes, it seemed increasingly likely I was well on my way to being mayor of the zone.

But we were good pals and she'd long since got used to my sense of humour.

So she wasn't offended when I arrived at her door in my little red sports car to invite her for the "top down, ride of her life", my having first checked the weather forecast for any chance of rain that afternoon in the greater Wandsworth area.

Chapter Six

I am a Rock. I am an Island.

"Those Ray-Bans do nothing for you, you know." Fiona said.

"Found them in the glove compartment. I guess the previous owner also had a Dustin Hoffman fixation."

"And all three of you are short. They made cars on the small side in the sixties, didn't they. Not much in the way of leg room," she said, trying to move the passenger seat back without success. I made a mental note that this was something I'd have to get fixed if Fiona was going to ride shotgun on a regular basis.

"Maybe people were smaller in the sixties. Smaller and groovier. Yeah, baby! Like Austin Powers… Who knows? I might have been very nearly average height back then."

"Very nearly."

"Anyway nobody looks good in Wayfarers. Except Jack Nicholson."

"I look spectacular in Wayfarers."

"Fiona, I think we established long ago that you look spectacular in most things."

"Including little red sports cars?"

"Them too."

It never ceased to surprise me that, gorgeous as Fiona was, she often went fishing for compliments. Maybe even beautiful people need validation or maybe she was just used to being complimented. I sometimes wondered if that was all beautiful people ever said to each other when they were together. Darling, you look wonderful this evening. Positively radiant. So do you, darling, your eyes are like the stars. That sort of thing.

"How's the racing car driver?" I asked.

"James Hunt?"

I'd been Fiona's platonic companion once more the previous week when, as usual, a number of more or less eligible men came on to Fiona, every man Jack of them entirely dismissing the possibility that I might actually be Fiona's date. One of the more persistent Tarzan lookalikes was indeed called James, did indeed drive racing cars for a living, and did indeed bear a passing resemblance to Britain's blonde-Norse-God-like Formula One champion from the 1970s. He hadn't offered his last name when he first approached, no doubt hoping he was sufficiently famous we would recognise him, so I had taken to calling him Hunt. Rhyming slang intended.

"We went out for dinner," Fiona said. "I had to fight him off at the door when we said good night so I think Mr Hunt's quite likely to turn into Mr Rhyming Slang... Oh look... deer."

"What, dear?"

I'd decided Richmond Park was the most suitable venue for the car's test drive since it wasn't too far from home if it broke down and we needed a tow. It's also the closest thing South London has to a drive in the country without fighting your way through traffic to get out of London and into something that could genuinely be called countryside.

"Who owns them, I wonder?" Fiona asked. "They must belong to someone."

"The Queen, I assume. It's a Royal Park, so the Queen, I guess. It'll be rutting season soon."

"For who? The Queen or the deer?"

"For whom, dear, for whom… The deer, of course. I think the closest the Queen comes to rutting these days is watching the corgis dry humping the staff."

"One of life's simple pleasures."

"Like inbreeding and roasting peasants in front of an open fire."

"Pheasants?"

"No… Peasants."

"How about you, Ben? Have you rutted lately?"

"What do you think?"

"I know what I think, but I thought it polite to ask anyway. Aren't you more eligible now? Surely you're something of a catch. Lottery winner seeks gold digging redhead."

"You've seen my ad in the paper then. No, I prefer blondes."

"Aren't you sweet."

"Maybe I *should* advertise. Is internet dating socially acceptable now?"

"I haven't the slightest idea."

"No, you probably don't."

'I think I've had enough of men for now."

"How many is that now?"

"None of your business."

"How do you feel about corgis?"

"Horrid little things."

"I could always dry hump your leg for a bit until something better comes along."

"I'll let you know. Does the radio work?"

"Only gets Radio 2."

"Then I'll have to do make do with that."

She turned the knob and fiddled with the tuning. Satisfied that it did only get Radio 2 she turned up the volume.

"I like this one."

Simon and Garfunkel. *The Sound of Silence*. She turned the volume up as loud as it would go without crackling through the speakers, also a little cracked from too many hours of top-down sunshine.

"Ben, did you ever think that your hero in that film, the guy you named yourself after, is just some crazy stalker who thinks he's in love with some girl he hardly knows?"

"But aside from that, Mrs Lincoln, how did you like the show?"

"Just thought I'd ask… Can I borrow your sunglasses, Ben? The sun's in my eyes."

"Keep them. They make me look like a dick."

Chapter Seven

And a Rock Feels No Pain.

"How's the new car?" Stuart asked.

"In the garage. Broke down after I dropped Fiona off. Apparently it doesn't like the rain."

"Hey, it's Italian. What are you going to buy next? Leather trousers?"

"Are they waterproof?"

"I expect so. Cows are. Another pint?"

"Why not."

"Guinness again?"

"Sure, why not."

We were in the Slug and Lettuce near Victoria Station. Not nearly as nice as the old Slug and Lettuce but Stuart fancied the barmaid, which at least meant that he hadn't ducked out to the gents every time it was his round.

As a general rule I prefer traditional pubs. I don't mind new and shiny in a restaurant but pubs should be old. A bit worn and tatty at the edges. I went to university in Dublin back in the 1980s when the whole city looked old and frayed at the edges. I went there for no better reason than I liked Guinness and heard that it tasted better there. It did. And nowhere did they pour a better pint of Guinness than in the tatty old pubs that hadn't seen a lick of paint since James Joyce drank there.

I studied English and Drama at Trinity College. That and Guinness. In my last year I had rooms in college. I believe a student fired a shot at the British troops out of my window during the Easter Uprising in 1916. Or was it from the room above me? No one seemed to know for sure. Not a hotbed for revolutionary activity, Trinity College, then or now. The sniper was probably one of the few students there who wasn't British. The university was always a haven for West Brits as they were called, the Brits who didn't quite get into Oxford. And an Irish friend told me that right up to 1972 you could be excommunicated if you were Roman Catholic and you went to Trinity.

My father never berated me for giving up the chance to study at Oxford, but truth be told I probably wouldn't have passed the entrance exam and the weekend I took the train down to check out the city of dreaming spires every college seemed to be full of ex-public school types. At the time I fancied myself as something of a working class hero, though I was neither working class nor in any way heroic. Middle class and ordinary. That's me.

If Oxford had been my father's ambition for me, he accepted my choice of Dublin with good grace, perhaps because he had briefly studied there as part of his medical degree. Midwifery it was, I think, he studied in Dublin. Do doctors study midwifery as part of their education or is it just midwives? I'm not sure but I'm fairly certain he spent his time in Dublin more studiously than I did.

I switched from English and Philosophy to English and Drama after one week because an Irish friend already on that course told me that Drama Studies was a "feckin' doss" and first week Philosophy had turned out to be a good deal harder than I'd imagined. When I had thought of going to Oxford it had been my foolish ambition to study PPE. God knows what I would have made of Politics and Economics given that my study of Philosophy lasted one solitary lecture and a chapter on Descartes. I think therefore I... will study drama instead because it's got to be easier than this. It was.

Johnny, my much smarter chum from school did in fact go to Oxford, did study philosophy and did do a PHD, though not at Oxford. He's now a Professor of Philosophy in Sydney, Australia, of all places where it's famously "hot enough to boil a monkey's bum". You see, I can never think about Johnny without recalling the Monty Python sketch where everyone's called Bruce in the Philosophy Department of the University of Walamalloo. I hadn't seen Johnny since school so for all I know he might have changed his name to Bruce "just to keep things simple" and who knows? He might also be "in charge of the sheep dip". There but for the grace of God went I. No, that was never likely to happen.

I spent my four years in Dublin less productively than John at Oxford. I chose one course on the American novel for no better reason that I had a crush on Peggy

O'Brien, the American lecturer, who was tall and graceful and sophisticated in a New England waspish kind of way. I was amazed when I was told that she'd had a girlish crush on the poet, Brendan Kennelly, a lecturer at Trinity; Peggy, a student in his class. He was neither tall, nor graceful, nor sophisticated, and a famously ferocious drinker. When I first saw him, still teaching at the university, bumbling across the quad with two plastic bags stuffed full of I know not what, I mistook him for a tramp looking for a quiet place to sleep.

There's a story that his doctor told him that if he didn't stop drinking he'd be dead in a year. Brendan's response was 'I'll have to think about it. A man can drink a hell of a lot in a year'. But undergraduate Peggy fell for his peculiar charms and it must have been love because they were married for seventeen years.

One of of his longer pieces of verse is called *Poetry My Arse,* which I think tells you all you need to know about him as a man and as a poet. As a university lecturer, all I can tell you is that most of his seminars were taught across the road from the college in the snug at O'Neill's, traditionally the haunt of poets and liars, or The Stag's Head, a favourite pub of James Joyce and also my good friends, Maura and Amy. And me. Another excellent place to order a Guinness and talk about anything other than literature.

They had a daughter I was told, Peggy and Brendan. They called her Doodle. Perhaps he was struggling to write a poem about his arse and doodling around the time of her conception, I don't know. I think Peggy went back to Massachusetts to teach at Amherst, where I imagine she truly belongs. She was also a published poet although I'm guessing she never wrote about her arse, which was a shame, since I, for one, remember it as being the stuff of poetry and I'm sure I wasn't alone.

I doubt if she remembers me as one of her better students, although I still have a preference for American writers. They have a more playful attitude to language, something they share with the Irish. So I now regret that at Trinity I perversely avoided anything to do with Irish literature and James Joyce in particular, except for seeking out his favourite watering holes to wet my whistle. You could pay to go on literary pub tours back then and probably still can, though I doubt it's high on the list of things to do for those on the countless stag do's that now are spent drinking in Dublin. I'm guessing most of them seek out a Wetherspoons or some other ghastly chain of generic pubs. To be fair I never went on one of those literary tours either. I thought the tour guide might start spouting Joyce at me.

I imagine a lot of the old pubs in Dublin I frequented are Wetherspoons now, full of drunken English guys on stag do's or else they've been turned into brasseries or bistros since Dublin became drunk on money from Brussels and the EEC in the 1990s. Great news for all those lucky Dubs who were already on the housing ladder, bad news for anyone who wasn't. Plus ça change… I think Mulligan's is still there, one of my favourite watering holes and a bit off the beaten track. I'd deliberately sought it out because it had been one of my dad's old haunts when he studied at the Rotunda Hospital.

Stuart returned with two pints of Guinness, neither one of which would have passed muster in a Dublin pub. Not even in a Wetherspoons.

"She can't pull much of pint, can she?" I said as Stuart sat down.

"Yes, but look at her."

"She's young enough to be your daughter."

"I'll try not to let thought that get in my way."

"I never saw anyone take so long to pull a pint of Guinness to so little effect". The pint tasted as thin as it looked, which is not a good look and not a good taste if you're a pint of Guinness.

"Any thoughts on how you're going to spend your ill-gotten gains? After you've bought a pair of leather trousers, I mean."

"Maybe I should go the whole hog. Have a mid-life crisis, the whole nine yards. While I still have time left."

"You're not still harping on about that psychic, are you?"

"He was right about the lottery. I was thinking about something earlier. Remember the guy who stayed in the next door room to me at Trinity? Harry. I think you met him when you came over for the rugby in my final year."

"I remember we got our arses kicked by the Irish. Couldn't even get tickets because of the prices the scalpers were asking. Greedy little bastards. We had to watch the game in a bar."

"Harry was English. Tall and thin and dead posh. Posher than posh. Posh like Prince Charles posh."

"Vaguely. Did he have big ears?"

"I really don't remember, but the thing is Harry told me this story about a guy who was at Trinity in his father's time. And this guy won the Irish lotto or something… No, not the lotto, he got some huge inheritance he wasn't expecting. An uncle died without kids or something. So all of a sudden this guy's not just rich. He's Richy O'Rich rich, absolutely loaded, and he decides to go out on the rip to celebrate. Now apparently this guy didn't have many mates. A bit like Harry as a matter of fact. But word gets out and there's suddenly no shortage of friendly undergrads who are more than happy to help him celebrate his good fortune and off they all pop to the pub, but the problem was this guy, Billy No Mates, isn't much of a drinker so after a while he just leaves some money on the bar to cover the tab and totters off to go back to his room all by his lonesome, 'cos his new mates ain't leaving while there's cash on the bar and pints to be drunk. So this guy's staggering home alone and that was the last mistake he ever made."

"How come?"

"He stepped out in front of a bus. End of story. Stone dead. Died on the spot. Never got a chance to spend the rest of his inheritance. True story. According to Harry."

"All the more bloody reason to get up off your arse and start living it up a bit."

"So live fast, die young, leave a good looking corpse?"

"Not sure you've got the makings of a good looking corpse. I should think long and hard about having an open coffin."

"I'm planning on being cremated."

"It's your funeral."

"Cremation it is."

"Look on the bright side. At least you'll be warm . You were were never much of a hottie in life. Ugly and rich is better than plain old ugly."

"There's a comfort. So live fast in the meantime. That's the extent of your good advice."

"Why don't you put on a play?"

"I think I'm done with all that acting stuff."

"You don't have to act. You could direct. You weren't half bad at that when you directed the show we did together."

"He said, damning with faint praise."

"You hate the job you're doing."

"It pays the rent."

For a few years I'd been scraping a living working freelance as a technical writer. I got the idea when I was re-reading Robert M Pirsig's *The Art of Motorcycle Maintenance*, which is a fantastic book that I warmly recommend you read if you haven't already, something I cannot say about anything I've worked on as a technical writer. I have actually co-written a pamphlet of Zen Buddhism and edited a manual on motorcycle maintenance but I'm not much cop at transcendental meditation or handling a monkey wrench for that matter. So I can't say my heart was ever in my latest career and I wasn't very good at it, hence why I was still working freelance and barely scraping together the rent every month.

"Paying the rent is not something you have to worry about for a while. And you should start looking for a better place than that hovel you're living in. You could get yourself quite a swanky little bachelor's pad now. Invite girls up to look at your etchings."

"Never worked when I was a student. I had a painting by one of the modernists, the genuine article. The college had a huge art collection and not enough space to hang them all, so they would loan them out to you if you had rooms in college. All you had to do was pay ten quid for insurance. Pretty good deal for the loan of a masterpiece and I loved having it, but not once did I get a girl up to my room to look at it. In fact it was so useless as a fanny magnet that I can never remember the name of the guy who painted the damn thing. I think it began with an M."

"You've got enough cash to be your own producer now."

"Mark something… or was it the French spelling? Marc with a c… I think he was Russian but it's a French name… It sounds French."

"Stop changing the subject."

"I think he was one of the surrealists. Or was he a cubist, like Picasso? I was never totally sure. Anyway there was a bunch of fish and this strange looking woman coming out of the sea."

"Come on, you've got a bunch of plays already written that were never produced which were pretty damn good, I thought. And please note there was nothing faint about that bit of praise."

"Chagall. That was the guy's name"

"That starts with a C not an M."

"Marc Chagall."

"Fantastic. You've remembered his name. Now we can all die happy. Now stop changing the subject and answer my question."

"I'm sorry. I've just had Dublin on my mind. I was wondering if that's where it all started to go wrong. If I'd never gone to Dublin I'd never have gone into acting in the first place."

"I'm waiting… If you don't answer the damn question you're going to be wearing that pint of Guinness."

"What a tragedy that would be."

"I'll tell you what would be a tragedy. You passing up on an opportunity that literally just fell in your lap. That would would be a tragic waste of whatever. Don't forget the money made by the Lottery was all originally supposed to go into funding the arts. So stop pissing about, get off the pot and bloody well fund them."

"Oh, I dunno… You go to all the trouble of putting together a show and nobody ever comes."

"You could hire a decent venue for once. Not like those shit-hole pub theatres we used to act in. Get yourself some decent publicity. People would come. I'm not talking the West End and cast of thousands. It doesn't have to be Les Miserables but you've got the cash to put on something worth watching. Finally put on a show… now I know I'm going to regret saying this, but here goes… Finally put on a show that's worthy of the the material."

"Meaning one of my scripts?"

"Sure. Why not? Let's take that old barn and turn it into a theatre."

"Oh gee, Linus, do ya think we could? Golly, wouldn' that be somethin'?"

"Yes, Charley Brown. Why the hell not?"

"Let's drink to that. Let's raise our glasses to 'why the hell not'."

"Seriously? You'll do it? No just thinking about it and then not doing it."

"I'll think about it."

Long meaningful conversations were never a big feature of my friendship with Stuart. Generally compliments went unpaid, affection left unexpressed. So the topic of conversation returned to more usual areas for us. Sarcasm and sport, namely the seeming impossibility of Scotland ever having a strong enough team to kick some poetic Irish arse and win the Six Nations again, let alone the World Cup.

So while we talked of many things though not of cabbages and kings or whether pigs indeed have wings, Stuart's notion of putting on one of my plays stayed with me. Part of my mind wandered down the proverbial wonderland burrow while Stuart rabbited on about rugby. It didn't actually sound like such a terrible idea. I *was* thinking about it until Stuart interrupting my thinking about it.

"Another Guinness?"

"I'll get it. It's my round."

"No, I'll get it."

"It must be love. Or something like it. Give her my regards or better still my phone number."

"You find your own barmaid."

"I might try a pint of Murphy's this time. See if she can pour a decent pint of that. Or something like it."

"It won't be any better."

"Is that like Murphy's Law? Anything that can go wrong with pulling a pint of stout will inevitably go wrong?"

"Only one way to find out." Stuart picked up the empty glasses and went off to resume his attempted seduction of the barmaid.

Guinness or Murphy's Irish Stout. I could never quite finally decide on which one I liked better. Usually if I see a pub sells Murphy's I start with a pint of that and stick with it if it tastes anything like it should, because just about every pub in the country sells Guinness and usually in two varieties, regular and that ghastly chilled stuff. I think it all comes from the same keg. It's just that one of them comes out colder like a pint of lager. James Joyce would be turning in his grave.

I sometimes thought of going back to Dublin for a visit although the only time I did fly over for a weekend I'd fallen out with my old friend, Bryan, who'd been in the same year as me studying Drama and, by the time I returned to visit, had established himself as a moderately successful theatre director and a complete arse. He had a show on at the Abbey Theatre and spent the whole evening chasing the female lead, who'd also been at Trinity at the same time as us.

I don't know whether Bryan pulled or not because, feeling bored and a little ignored because, fair do's, I had flown over for the weekend after all, halfway back on my return from the Gents I thought 'fuck it' and walked out, pulling my collar up against the Dublin night and doing my best I don't care, James-Dean-walking-in the-rain-through-Times-Square number, and trudged back to my lonely hotel room. Truth be told I wasn't just pissed off at Bryan for ignoring me. I was a little jealous.

I had a vague memory of failing to get off with the same girl at a party in college and getting drunk instead. Plus ça change… And she was a nice girl. Just not my girl. Are we beginning to see a pattern here? I think so. Not getting the girl and getting drunk instead. Maybe James Joyce would be proud of me after all. I was turning into a first rate Leopold Bloom. Siobhan was her name. Boyishly pretty with red hair and therefore perfect casting for Pegeen Mike in the *Playboy of the Western World,* which was what Bryan was directing her in. Some years later I saw a posting on Facebook that said she'd died very young. Still in her twenties, I think. Sad. Very sad.

"Oh, my grief, I've lost him surely; I've lost the only Playboy of the Western World."

Nice girl. Dreadful play.

Bryan with a 'y'. What an arse.

Stuart was on his way back. One more pint and I wasn't going to be feeling any pain at all. Or anything else for that matter. I picked up a menu off the table, thinking it might be a good idea to see if the food was any better than the beer. Where was a bistro or a brasserie when you needed one? Or even a Wetherspoons for that matter.

Chapter Eight

Feeling No Pain at All

Feeling no pain at all can sometimes seem like quite a good idea. However, on almost all of these occasions it turns out to be a very bad idea indeed.

And true to form on this occasion it was nearly a very, very bad idea since, just as we were leaving the bar a couple of pints later, I stepped out in front of a bus. Fortunately Stuart was there to save me.

Chapter Nine

The Wheels on the Bus

It's a funny thing but coincidences actually do happen in real life, which leaves you wondering if God has a sense of humour.

Example. Shakespeare and Cervantes died on the exact same day. Same year, same month, same day. Maybe both died at exactly the same time. Just after breakfast perhaps or at four in the morning, statistically the most like time to die. It's also the best time to make a night attack. That's when your enemy is at his doziest or statistically most likely to die anyway. Four in the morning is the time when you are normally experiencing your deepest sleep. Or death. But who would have guessed that seemingly unlikely coincidence? Indisputably the greatest writer in the English language, the creator of Lear and Hamlet and Romeo and Juliet, dying on the same day as the man who came up with Don Quixote and tilting at windmills and, in doing so, invented the novel, in a book that's been translated into more languages than any other apart from the Bible.

I never got past the first chapter of big Don Q (it's very long) when it was on the reading list for a course on the early novel in Dublin, but he's still a literary giant. So I don't claim to be standing on the shoulders of giants... Not like Sir Isaac Newton, born on Christmas day, same as... no, not him. Shepherds don't watch their flocks or wash their socks by night for that matter. Not out of doors in Bethlehem in December they don't. It's too damn cold. No, Christmas day, same as Humphrey Bogart and a surprising number of very famous cricketers. Shakespeare and Miguel de Cervantes... dying on the same day...

Coincidence? Si, Señor.

And something related and coincidental by way of literary deaths happened to me when I lived in a small village in Scotland called Blackford. It's just south of Gleneagles Hotel, the swanky place with two golf courses. Maybe you watched the Ryder Cup when they staged it there in 2014. Or perhaps you remember it was where Tony Blair was hosting the G8 summit nine years before and had to fly to London on the day it was awarded the Olympics because of the terrorist bombs planted in the city earlier that day. London's 7/7 as it became known. Makes Blackford sound quite a groovy place to live, doesn't it? Just down the road from Scotland's premier hotel.

Si, Señor? No, Señor.

Don't ever go there. It's always raining. It can be lovely and sunny two miles up the road at Gleneagles and chucking it down in Blackford. You might have tried the mineral water they bottle there, Highland Spring. Never any shortage of water in Blackford. Local legend has it that the village was named the Black Ford after the unfortunate demise of "the Fair Queen Helen", wife of the Viking King, Magnus Olaffson, known to his friends as Magnus Barefoot or Magnus Bare Legs. She drowned while fording the river. I think there are about a dozen places called Blackford in the UK and I'll bet there all rubbish, completely pants, miserable places to live.

If you're wondering why they called him Magnus Bare Legs it's because, to make up for all the raping and pillaging he did in Scotland, he took to wearing the local dress, a short tunic that daringly showed off bit of leg. It's thought to be the forerunner of the kilt. A sort of early attempt to win hearts and minds when he was done hacking off the locals' limbs.

The only good thing I can say about the village is that it had a great little pub. Not the ghastly mock Tudor place on the main street. I'm talking about The Blackford Inn on Stirling Street. I lived just across the road and they did a fabulous steak dinner, so I spent many a happy evening there. And one evening in early May 2000 I walked in there to see they had started a Dead Pool, a sort of winner takes all sweepstakes, where you picked the names of a couple of ageing celebrities and if your horse died first, as it were, you won all the cash in the pot.

I thought this sounded a bit of a lark, albeit a touch morbid, and I liked the Clint Eastwood movie of the same name. So I thought 'what the hell?' I was one of the last of the locals to go in on the Dead Pool so there weren't many runners and riders left to choose from.

"Who's left?" I asked the barman who was also the owner and head chef. It's a very small pub and not at all like a Wetherspoons.

"Not much of a selection, I'm afraid. Just a couple of old dears left."

"That's okay. I'm not very good at making decisions, especially if they're life and death ones."

"I can give you Sir John Gielgud and Dame Barbara Cartland."

A world famous actor and a writer of sorts seemed a perfect choice to me as the world's least famous actor and also a writer. Of sorts.

"That'll do nicely. American Express?"

"Cash only for the Dead Pool."

The barman put my fiver in a large glass jar sitting under the pool of death on the wall.

"How much is in there?"

"Haven't counted it. About a hundred and fifty, I should think."

"Salman Rushdie wrote the 'that'll do nicely' advert for American Express, you know. Back when he worked as a copywriter. Not a lot of people know that."

"Not a lot of people care. Guinness?"

"That'll do nicely."

Imagine my surprise when two weeks later on the twenty-first of May in the first year of the new millennium both my horses fell at the first fence. Sir

John and Dame Barbara popped their clogs on the same day.

I couldn't believe it and as you can imagine I felt a bit guilty. I was a huge fan of Sir John though not Dame Barbara. It felt like I'd given both of them the kiss of death. Of all the people in all the world, of all the the people in the Blackford Inn Dead Pool, not just one of the people I'd picked but both of them had died on the the exact same day.

By predicting their deaths had I in fact somehow caused their demise? I felt like one of the triumvirate in Shakespeare's *Julius Caesar*, making a list of *"who shall live and who shall die"*.

"These many, then, shall die; their names are prick'd."

Act IV, Scene I.

And a bit of a prick is how I'd felt all afternoon after I heard the lunchtime news. Poor old Gielgud...

I thought of all the wonderful performances he had given in so many classic theatre roles. Gielgud, one of the famous triumvirate of the British stage, Olivier, Richardson and Gielgud. He was Romeo, he was Hamlet, he was Prospero...

"Our revels now are ended. These our actors,
As I foretold you, were all spirits and
Are melted into air, into thin air:
And, like the baseless fabric of this vision,
The cloud-capp'd towers, the gorgeous palaces,
The solemn temples, the great globe itself,
Yea, all which it inherit, shall dissolve
And, like this insubstantial pageant faded,

Leave not a rack behind. We are such stuff
As dreams are made on, and our little life
Is rounded with a sleep."

Yes, a bit of a prick is what I felt like. And yet, and
yet… Gielgud. He'd probably be remembered by
most people for what he said to Dudley Moore in the
movie, *Arthur*.
"You little shit!" said a voice behind me,
coincidentally, as I walked in to collect my winnings
on that evening. One of the regulars was sat opposite
me in a corner beside the Dead Pool. "I'll bet you
cheated."
"How could I cheat? Do you think I hired a hitman or
popped down to London for the day to knock them
both off?"
"Bloody suspicious if you ask me. Both of them
dying on the same day."
"I think you should pay me double. It's a
whatchamacallit. An accumulator. If I'd made that bet
with Ladbrokes I'd have won a small fortune."
"I still think it's bloody iffy."
"It's just a coincidence," I said. "Nothing to do with
me at all."
So, you see coincidences do happen. Like me
stepping out in front of that bus.
Because the woman driving the bus was… a complete
stranger.
No, the coincidence was that I'd stepped out in front
of a bus on my way home from the pub. Just like the

poor sod in Harry's story who died just after inheriting a pile of money from his uncle. Suddenly come into some money. Just like me. I'd likewise just received a huge amount of unexpected cash and was also, don't forget, under a sentence of death.

The wheels of God grind slowly, yet grind exceeding small. Or whatever the saying is.

Thank God for Stuart for grabbing hold of my arm just before the wheels of the bus found me and ground me exceeding small.

Chapter Ten

And this Rock Does Feel Pain

The next morning I woke up feeling quite a lot of pain at both ends. A twisted ankle and a blinding headache. Two unwelcome results of drinking too much Guinness. And Murphy's. My head felt heavy as a rock, only a rock feels no pain. But it was better than any of the possible alternatives. Like being run over by a bus and waking up in Intensive Care. Or not waking up at all.

So I lay there trying to keep very still while I considered how close I'd come to death the day before and wondering what fate lay in store for me if the Great Alfonso's second prediction were to prove correct. An accident in or near the home seemed the most probable. Drowning, electrocution, falling from a ladder or some sort of traffic accident being just a few of the possibilities I came up with. Getting hit by an asteroid or struck by lightning were not impossible but seemed unlikely and I thought I was pretty safe from an earthquake or a tsunami so long as I avoided foreign travel.

There are of course any number of obscure and even stupid ways to die as recognised by the Darwin

Awards, given to those who manage to eliminate themselves from the gene pool in spectacularly stupid ways. They were invented by a bunch of smarty pants at various universities back in the 1980s who inhabited chat rooms on something called the Usenet which pre-dated the world wide web by a number of years.

If death was imminent and my time was limited maybe Stuart was right. Was it time to get off the pot and take a piss? I did in fact need a piss but whenever I lifted my head it felt like my cranium stayed where it was and my brain moved inside it.

It was not a good feeling. Death might have come as a happy release.

So I continued to lie there trying to keep very still and considered Stuart's idea of putting on a play. A resumption of my dormant acting or directing and playwriting careers. Did I really want to go back down that road again? I remembered the urban myth about Einstein's definition of madness; doing the same thing over and over again expecting different results. Ironically the first record of anyone actually saying that dates back only to the 1980s and it's from one of those twelve step programs like Alcoholics Anonymous. The irony was certainly not lost on me at that moment.

Where was an aspirin when you needed one? Or a meteor shower? Or a tsunami? Anything to save me from the earthquake in my head.

Chapter Eleven

Popping the Corky

I said that I've sometimes wondered what would have happened if I hadn't gone to Dublin. I certainly would not have become an actor. Maybe you're one of those people whose life goes perfectly to plan. Perhaps you once read a self-help book that says soothing words of encouragement like 'if you want something badly enough you can make it happen'. Or perhaps you even wrote the book.

Fiona's a bit like that. True, she wanted to perform herself when she was a young up-and-coming ballerina before her teenage up-and-up-ing growth spurt put a stop to all that. She quickly realised that teaching ballet was far more lucrative and less damaging to your body than actually being a prima ballerina yourself. And she's pretty happy with that. She likes money. She likes having nice clothes and a nice flat and there's nothing wrong with that.

It probably sounds like I'm saying there's something bad about being motivated by money. I'm not. I'm just saying that money isn't what motivates me. It's probably me who's the dummy, the impractical one, the dreamer, not her. Fiona's one of those lucky people who's basically pretty happy with life apart from the fact that she hasn't found Mr Right. But she's never without Mr Right Now for long, so it's probably just a matter of time.

That's not how things go for me. If I was motivated by money I'd probably have thought long and hard about becoming an actor. It's a hell of a precarious way of making a living for most of us. But I didn't think long and hard about it. More's the pity.

I came to the conclusion some time ago that almost every major decision I've made in life has been a mistake. If there's a wrong way to go, I'll find it or rather it will find me.

Example: by the time I got to my last year at university I'd done a fair amount of acting and a number of Dublin theatre professionals had said nice things and implied I might have what it takes to act professionally. Now even then I knew that nine out of ten actors are out of work nine tenths of the time and that the lucky tenth actor gets nine out of ten of the best jobs going. So I sat down for a coffee with the man in charge of what was then Dublin's only acting school for a bit of counselling on whether I was wise to think of acting by way of a career. Michael Joyce was his name. No relation to James as far as I know. "Basically, I think you're quite talented." was his opening remark.

Just the sort of encouragement I needed, no? There was me worrying he might be a little vague about my prospects. He went on to recommend a couple of acting schools in London and one in Bristol where he had taught that I might like to apply to. This was back in the day when there were only a small number of specialist schools training actors before dozens of universities began running four or five acting courses, acting for film, acting for the stage, Shakespearean acting and so on as well as numerous creative writing courses covering everything from writing screenplays to composing origami poetry on coloured paper in the shape of a butterfly. Yes, really. I saw the butterflies, didn't bother to read the poetry. I expect it was Haikus or blank verse. Can't remember who said it but writing blank verse is like playing tennis without a net.

So I auditioned for the three acting schools he recommended and got accepted by one of them, which luckily was the only one in the country to get funding from local government and cost only a small fraction of what I would have had to pay otherwise. The funding's long since disappeared and my old drama school now costs the same as all the rest. Ever wondered why so many famous British actors are really posh? It's because going to drama school is really expensive.

So I didn't really choose acting as a career. It chose me. I left the decision up to fate. If I hadn't been accepted at drama school that year I wouldn't have tried again and I'd never have started acting or become a playwright, which I only ever started because I could never get work as an actor. Writing plays for me and Stuart seemed like a marginally better use of my time than doing nothing while waiting for the phone to ring.

What was drama school like? Mostly movement and voice classes in the morning, rehearsals for a play in the afternoon. Four plays a term with the class year split in two different casts rehearsing two different plays at any one time. So it was my second year there before I really got to know two of my better friends from that time. I'd hardly spoken a word to Thomasina in first year and then we got cast as lovers in the next play.

Now Thomasina, like Fiona, was tall and blonde. Much taller than me. For a while in her twenties she was the face and bubble-covered body in a bathtub for some Johnson & Johnson kind of product that gets you clean without drying out your epidermis. You possibly saw the ads. She had a baby in the bath with her in one of them. Not her baby. A stunt baby with a more successful career than me. I wonder who his agent was?

Now as you've probably gathered I'm not really leading man type material whether in real life or on stage. I'm pretty ordinary looking as I think I said before and so it was a bit daunting to be cast as the romantic lead in this scene, especially opposite Thomasina who was born to be a leading lady. Then there was the height difference and the fact that we'd barely spoken a word to each other in a year and a half. All this left me feeling a certain amount of trepidation. I was trying to comfort myself that I'd only have to play Captain Beefcake for one scene because at drama school they divide up the larger roles so that everyone has something to get their teeth into, when Thomasina, God bless her, walked straight up to me and said, "Come with me. We're going to the pub. I'm going to get to know you."

And get to know me she did. And in the end our scene wasn't half bad. We got past the height difference by Thomasina remaining seated throughout, me wearing cowboy boots and a ten gallon hat borrowed off Stuart from his gap year on a ranch in Texas, where incidentally the play was also set. So we avoided the danger of Thomasina standing in a trench like Shelley Winters opposite the famously diminutive actor, Alan Ladd, and we actually had a lot of fun rehearsing the first meeting of Corky Oberlander and Lu Ann Hampton Laverty (soon to be) Oberlander, since my character was destined to become her third husband somewhere between acts two and three in the play of the same name, *Lu Ann Hampton Laverty Oberlander*. Don't bother reading it. It's not a classic. So I managed my usual competent job and, like my dad I'm pretty good at accents and funny voices, so my Texas drawl was pretty accurate, thank y'all kindly, as was acknowledged by our acting tutor. His praise was tempered by his usual critique of my performance that I'd heard a couple of times before already. It was starting to sound like a refrain.

"We still need to get you past your habit of refrigerator acting". He meant I could have given the same performance opposite a refrigerator. But I still remember good ol' Corky with a certain fondness, if for no other reason that Thomasina and I became pretty good friends and that's how I acquired a certain liking for old style country music and Hank Williams in particular.

But the fact that I only appeared in Act Two meant that I never saw the girl rehearsing for the role of Lu Ann etc etc in Act Three until the set was complete on stage and we were running the whole play non-stop for the first time.

The moment Faith walked down the steps of her Texas ranch house to the strains of Patsy Cline singing "Crazy" and said her first words, something southern and inconsequential like "Well, I'll be darned", I was crazy in love, crazy for being so lonely, crazy for being so blue, crazy for loving you, Ms. Lu Ann Hampton Laverty Oberlander. I was feeling an achy breaky heart for Faith that I never felt onstage for Thomasina. I was simply captivated by Faith, seeing her act for the first time. She quite simply *was* Lu Ann Hampton Laverty Oberlander. Right away you felt you knew this woman. Knew all about her redneck, shit kickin' Texas childhood and her succession of failed marriages to redneck, shit kickin' cowboys. Faith was quite simply the most natural actor I'd ever seen. You can keep your De Niros and your Pacinos, your Streeps and your Blanchetts, none of them could hold a candle to this girl from South West London.

I'd never paid the slightest bit of attention to Faith before I saw her act on stage. Yes, she was sort of pretty but she was like Ingrid Bergman, not so beautiful in real life but captivating on stage or onscreen. I was smitten.

The next day our American director, who believed in method acting to the extent that if you weren't acting method you weren't acting at all, asked Faith and I to stay behind. The director explained she wanted Faith and me to do some work together so that Faith playing Lu Ann could draw on the emotional memory of being with Corky. But I knew this wasn't for Faith's benefit. This was all for me. And then the director said the words that always struck fear into my actor's heart.

"I want you to improvise…"

Improvisation. I hated it. And now I was being asked to open up emotionally with Faith, whom I barely knew but was now head over heels like a teenager in love with, the girl I'd seen on stage the day before. The director gave us the scenario. Corky had just come from Red's bar and they were fighting over how much time he spent there. Lu Ann was threatening to leave him if he didn't stop drinking. The drinking part should have been easy though this was way before Prozac had me turning semi-pro in the alcoholic stakes. More of that later. Let's stick to me making an arse of myself at drama school for now.

You see, acting drunk isn't that hard so it's strange you see it done so badly so often. The trick is not to act drunk but in fact to try very hard not to appear drunk, to play someone doing their level best to appear sober, because that's what people do unless they've reached the Weebles wobble but they don't fall down stage of drunk. And I was a tricksy sort actor so this slightly drunk part I could do.

I remember another student at drama school, nice guy, Indian origin, who'd never had a drink in his life. He asked me to explain what it felt like to be drunk. I said it was hard to explain what it felt like but playing it was easy. Quite why he sought my opinion on this I'm not sure. I'd like to think it was because we were friends rather than he thought I was a drunk. Back then I remember saying "two's my limit" in the pub in my best Texan drawl, which was a line from the play, though Corky never said it and I usually stayed for one more, just one for the road, since my walk home was a short one.

No, the hard part of the improv was the I love you, you don't really love me, that's why you're gonna leave me, go on, I dare y'all to walk out that door, I just dare ya' part of the improv. The trick to improvising, or so I've been told because I never mastered it, is listening. Listening and reacting to what you hear and never say no. Always go with what your improv partner gives you.

"Never say no to love" was this director's favourite expression. Her theory was that if at all possible your character's motivation should be love, even if their motivation appears to be anger or hate. And as tough for me as this was motivation-wise as someone who couldn't express love in real life, I could see where she was coming from with this mantra.

So drunk I could pull off. In love? Not so much.

The less said about the next thirty, yes, thirty minutes of unscripted fumbling without a script, improvising without a safety net, the better. Faith's performance was as effortless as before. Mine was abject. I was trying like hell to be open and to listen and react to what was in front of me, to what Faith was giving me and the harder I tried, the worse I got. I remember wishing it was Harry Dean Stanton playing Corky and not me. If you've seen him in *Paris, Texas,* you'll know why. Perhaps that was my first inkling that I would never be more than competent as an actor, at best a no nonsense meat and potatoes sort of actor. Like Anthony Hopkins without the talent. The nearest I ever got to fame was the day I walked into a pub in London and saw Helen Mirren snogging the face of Liam Neeson.

And within a few thoroughly disheartening years of leaving drama school I'd come to the conclusion that, if you were extraordinary in some way as an actor, beautiful, ugly, or blessed with a natural talent like Faith, you might, just might have a chance at making it as an actor. Unless of course you were well connected like Jennifer with a famous actress as a mother.

Jennifer and I were pretty close friends at drama school, I think because we were the same kind of actor. Too much head, not enough heart. Our only falling out was one night in the pub when she came out with the self pitying remark that it was tougher for her having a famous mother because you would be judged in a different way or some bullshit statement like that.

Well, folks, Jennifer left drama school a year early to make a television show playing her mother's daughter on screen and never spoke to me again. I heard from other friends from drama school that she never spoke to them either unless they got a part in a movie or in the West End and then a card or a call would come from Jennifer because all of a sudden they were friends worth having, friends that could help her further her career.

Jennifer's pretty famous now. You might not know her name, but you'd know her face. You've seen her in lots of movies, usually as the wife or mother, never the lead but always working, with a solid, seldom out of work for long in Hollywood sort of career.

In my more bitter, and for bitter read drunken, moments I used to fantasise about having one of my plays in the West End and inviting Jennifer in to read for a part and when she walked into the room I'd say "Sorry, luv, you're just not right for the role. We're looking for someone younger. And thinner..." Meow, saucer of milk for the bitch on table four.

What happened to Faith after drama school? Not me anyway. We had nothing really in common and I never had the nerve to tell her I loved her. She was dating a Welsh guy called Ian (spelt funny because he was Welsh) for most of the period I knew her. The last time I saw her she had a small part in a West End revival of *Separate Tables* with a couple of once famous has beens in the major roles.

I looked her up on Facebook a year or two ago and to judge by her profile she's happily married with a couple of kids. Not to Ian but to someone else and I remembered hoping she'd found a nice guy, someone who deserved to be with her. I sent her a Facebook message. She wrote back and said it was nice to hear from me after so many years. She said she still acted occasionally. A walk on part in *Eastenders* or whatever. She asked me how I was doing. I lied and said I was doing okay.

Now in the depths of my hangover I was thinking I could send her another message on Facebook. Tell her I was thinking of putting on a play and would she like to be in it. I wasn't in love with her any more so what could be wrong with that?

Chapter Twelve

Speaking in Tongues

I have the worst time making decisions. You know the old joke. I used think I was indecisive but now I'm not so sure. Not all that funny and neither is being indecisive. Maybe it comes from fear, the fear of taking the wrong path, not so much the path less travelled as the one that leads to the edge of the cliff. Some say indecision can be a symptom of depression. My dad said that as a teenager I completely skipped puberty and went straight on to menopause. Medically unlikely I know but he was a funny guy, my dad. Throughout my twenties doctors would tell me I should be on anti-depressants and eventually in a particularly low moment I let myself be persuaded to try Prozac. It wasn't called Prozac but that's what it was. This was at the time that the patent for Prozac proper was finished and doctors were prescribing the generic equivalent to just about anybody for just about anything. I read a statistic that said ten per cent of the population was taking it at one time. Okay, so that's not everyone but it's a hell of a lot of people. They couldn't all be suffering from clinical depression and nor I think was I.

I can only speak from my own experience but the happy pills didn't do much for me and had the unwelcome side effect that once I started drinking I didn't stop till I was unconscious, having first passed through the stage of being bitter, angry, aggressive and obnoxious to anyone who had the misfortune to be present. Or so I was told enough times to believe it and occasionally I could see such a trail of destruction the next morning to be convinced that me and Prozac were not a good match. The only pleasant side effect was that it strengthened and prolonged my erections but any requirement for these was truthfully speaking a rare event, as most of the time I was too drunk, angry, and obnoxious for an erection to be required.

Eventually I got off the Prozac though Lord knows it wasn't easy and I had to have a couple of go's at it. But it left me weakened with regards to self-control when it came to drinking especially when I was drinking alone. Perhaps it's like someone who's grown used to eating too much. They never feel like they've had enough until they've had too much.

On one famously drunken occasion, still very much on the Prozac, I ended up in the drunk tank at a police station and woke up the next day with no idea where I was, no idea how I'd got there, and a killer hangover to be informed that when they'd arrested me the previous night I'd refused to speak anything but French. Which was all very strange. For one thing I wasn't in France.

Now my French isn't all that good but I did do two seasons in the French Alps working as a ski bum and learned just enough French to get me into and out of trouble.

And here's a funny thing that I've never understood. I've always been pretty low on self-confidence when it comes to talking to girls, especially the ones I'd like to get close to. I don't have "the chat" as one of my female friends put it. Or even the brazen self-confidence bordering on sleaze that Stuart has that means he can chat up a barmaid young enough to be his daughter. The sort of in your face forwardness of someone I knew in college who would walk up to complete strangers at a party and ask them if they wanted to have sex. He got ignored most of the time and a lot of slaps in the face but I'm told he also had a lot of sex. A lot more than me to be sure. But the funny thing is, I'm generally a completely different person when I speak French. I'm confident, I'm charming. I'm forward.

I'm Pepe le Peu.

If you don't believe me, this is what happened to me one day when I was working in France. If you go to any ski resort in the French alps you'll see these municipal cops, we called them puppy cops, and they only work in the ski season. They're not proper cops. They're glorified traffic wardens is what they are, but at first glance they look like cops until you realise they're not packing heat.

And you wouldn't want them to be armed because in my experience they're almost all exclusively male, bad tempered, power crazy, proto-Nazis. And those are just the nicer ones. As part of my duties as a ski rep I occasionally had dealings with the local Chief of Police, usually because I'd got a parking ticket from a member of the Hitler youth. In contrast to the puppy cops, the head guy was always employed full time, year round, middle aged, stout, and could usually be placated by gifts of chocolate cake cooked by one of the chalet girls. But the rank and file puppy cops were pretty much all bastards to a man.

So imagine my surprise when I ran across an attractive young lady cop. And I was further surprised by what happened next. The conversation went something like this, with apologies if you don't speak French but if I wrote it in English you'd never believe it and you can use google translate for all I care or better still learn French because it's a beautiful language, the language of love. And if you do speak French, just remember I never claimed to be fluent in the first place.

"*Bonjour, mademoiselle. Tu es la plus belle gendarme dans les Hautes Alpes*".

No response from *La Belle Flic*. *Flic*, that's French slang for a cop. She just stops and stares. Probably wondering who the cheeky stranger with the funny accent is.

Thinking I had struck out and, a little embarrassed by my Maurice-Chevalier-skunk-type charm, I disappeared into the adjacent supermarket to buy a baguette. Paging Dr Freud… When I came out onto the street again she was still there. She hadn't moved. Emboldened, I continued.

"*Tu m'attend?*' I said.

"*Peut être...*"

"*Tu es vraiment très jolie, mademoiselle.*"

"*Merci, monsieur.*"

"*Je regrette que je ne travaille normalement pas dans cette ville. J'habite en Risoul.*"

There followed a short pause before her *réponse*.

"*Ce n'est pas si loins.*"

'*Sacré bleu',* I thought. I've just told her I live half an hour away on the other side of the mountain and she hasn't said "good for you", she's said "that's not so far…"

"*Peut-être tu veux parler avec moi* (my confidence and French still just about intact) *avec ta mobile?*"

"*Je ne sait pas ton numéro.*"

"*Maintenant tu sais. Tiens.*"

As requested she duly accepted my proffered business card with my British mobile number crossed out and my French work number written in its place that I had handy for just such an occasion. No, not really. But I did have a couple ready prepared in my wallet in case I needed to give someone my work number.

And that, boys and girls, is how I met Marie, *la belle flic*. We texted back and forth that evening, agreed to meet at 7pm the following day and as a gentleman I can't tell you what happened next, but let's just say we only drank a half glass of vin rouge before it was back to her place, a rather romantic open loft style apartment above the stables where Marie worked as a riding instructor in the summertime. And let's just say it was one of those rare occasions when I wished I was still on the Prozac. Giddy up....

True story, faithfully transcribed as far as my very happy memory of the occasion goes except for the fact that her French was *parfait, naturellement* so my apologies to any French scholars reading this for *mes erreurs de...* spelling and grammar.

Eat your heart out, Maurice Chevalier and Pepe le Peu for that matter.

Yes, borderline sleazy but I only had the balls to do it, if you'll pardon the pun, because I was speaking French. Yes, sometimes I did get the girl. Just not as often as I'd have liked.

What happened to Marie? The very next day I was transferred to another town to replace some clown who'd broken his leg snowboarding and had to be shipped back to Blighty. We kept in touch for a while, me and Marie, not the clown who broke his leg, but we were now many miles apart and while absence makes the heart fonder it doesn't half come as a kick in the teeth if you've just met a nice French girl. And so we never rode off together into the sunset on one of the horses I could hear occasionally whinnying or stamping their hooves on our one and only night of passion. And possibly in my dreams I hear them still. You know what they say. Unlucky at cards, lucky in love. Unfortunately I'm not much good at poker either.

Chapter Thirteen

Tongue Tied

Speaking in French I got the girl. I was bold. I was beautiful. I was *le Superman*

Back speaking English I was tongue tied and terminally indecisive. So what for others might be a simple decision like, you've got some money now, why not go with Stuart's suggestion and put together a show was met in my head with an endless round of ifs and ands. not needing tinkers' hands, leading to something akin to life plan paralysis.

Writers famously get writer's block and some famous writers found that the best way to get over it was to head for the drinks cabinet and go on a total bender. Top tip for writers: try not to do this and, if you must do it, stay the hell away from your laptop. That's the way laptops get broken. Keep them out of the reach of children and drunkards. There's also a danger of this becoming a habit and you'll find yourself completely unable to write without the aid of alcohol and what you end up writing won't make much sense or be any good at all. We can't all be Tennessee Williams and a drunk can do a lot more damage typing on a Macbook than on a Smith Corona

Another top tip if you're a writer and it's going well and writer's block is the furthest thing from your mind- keep a bottle of V8 veggie juice and a supply of hard-boiled eggs in the fridge- you can cut down lunch to 2 minutes and if you're truly stuck or blocked, you can always use the V8 veggie juice and vodka to make what I call a Vegan Vogon Bloody Mary, named after Douglas Adams' famously bad poet from the planet Vogon (patent pending, no Worcester sauce- it sometimes contains fishy stuff) and keep a jug of that in the fridge.

So I ignored my own advice on writers' block and life plan paralysis, poured my self a large one and had a good think about what to do next.

Chapter Fourteen

A Writer Gets Unblocked

Somewhere in the middle of my third, very large Vegan Vogon Bloody Mary I came to an epiphany. It wasn't a religious experience along the lines of Moses and the Burning Bush or Saul on the road to Damascus but… What got burned there? I forget? Was it his donkey?

I read somewhere that religious revelations come to some people with epilepsy when they're having a seizure. Something to do with increased activity in their lobes or their left prefrontal cortex or whatever that actually does show up on medical scans in the same area as those not so afflicted but who still claim to have religious visions or to be talking to God. Maybe the same is also true of people who are a bit drunk in the brief period when life seems to suddenly make sense, when everything falls into place, just before they get a bit more drunk and stop making sense altogether. And the trick on these occasions is to have pen and paper handy to write down your sudden insight. That and to try to write as legibly as you can. What I came up with was this. If, as predicted on my birthday, I had a limited time left on the planet, maybe I should stop worrying about what time I had left and do something worthwhile with that time, however much I had left. Not much of a revelation I know but I came up with something more concrete as well.

I reckoned I could go either one of two ways and, as is fairly common with people on the way to getting a bit drunk, I decided now was a very good time to make a phone call and tell someone about it.

"Stuart, I've come up with a relevation... Revelation..."

"Have you been drinking?"

"Just a bit... Listen, I can't find a piece of pen and paper so this is what I've come up with. I've got a plan, well not so much a plan as two different ones. Two ideas."

"Go on, I'm listening." I could have sworn I heard a near inaudible sigh coming down the phone at me but I continued, undaunted.

"Have you got a pen and paper handy, Stuart? This is important."

"No, but I haven't got a drink handy either so I'll probably remember what your big-thing-plan is."

"Plans... Two plans. Plan number one. *Numero uno...* Take up a hobby."

"Brilliant."

"Thank you. You're very kind."

"Is that it?"

"No, that's not it. There's more..."

"Oh good."

"Remember that Monty Python sketch the one where different contestants have to summarise Proust's masterpiece, *A la Recherche de Temps Perdu?* Once in a swimsuit and once in evening dress…"

"Yes, I remember. Good to hear all those nights we spent in Stockwell listening to Monty Python records wasn't a complete waste of time. This conversation on the other hand…"

"And the different contestants included Omar Sharif and Yehudi Menuhin and various members of the all conquering Surrey cricket team of the 1950's…"

"Please, don't name them all. I'm begging you."

"And the quiz master guy is introducing the first contestant and he asks him if he has any other hobbies apart from Proust summarising and he says…"

"Strangling animals, golf, and masturbation. Yes, I remember. Is this conversation going anywhere?"

"Well, it occurred to me that I've already tried two of those."

"And I'd say you've pretty much mastered one of them."

"I'm no longer king of the castle, master of my own domain, very good. *Seinfeld.* Excellent episode. One of my favourites, the one where the four of them have to refrain from bashing the bishop or double clicking her mouse in Elaine's case. Anyway it occurred to me that I could take up a hobby."

"Strangling animals?"

"No, golf."

"You can already play golf."

"Not very well. I thought I could get better."

"And that's it, is it? Your big revelation… Play more golf."

"I haven't told you about my other plan. Plan number two."

"I'm all ears."

"I'm going to take your advice and put on a play. And I know which one. The one we were going to do together but didn't have any money. Only now I've got plenty of money and I know how to make it better… how to fix it, the ending. It's just come to me how to make it better."

"I'm very glad to hear it."

"And I've got a new title, a better one."

"Which is?"

"*Live Fast, Dai Young*"

"That's what it was before."

"No, before it was *Live Fast, Die Young*. It's a pun, like David but in Welsh, *Dai,* do you see?"

"No, it must be a visual one. Send me an email."

"Good idea. I'll do that tomorrow. In the meantime I need you to find a pen and a piece of paper to write all this down before I forget it all."

"Believe me, there's no way I'm going to forget this conversation before tomorrow. It's burned into my memory."

"Okay, just remember. *Dai Young* like the Welsh name *Dai* and that I don't commit suicide at the end of the play. You kill me."

"I'm liking this idea better all the time."

"Attaboy, Stu. You're a pal."

"Yes, I am. And, Ben?"

"Yes?"

"Don't drink too much in the meantime… Oh, and just one more word of advice…"

"What's that?"

"If you go outside. Look left, look right, and watch out for double decker buses."

"That's excellent advice."

"And don't forget to wash your hands."

Chapter Fifteen

In Vino Veritas

Not all writers reach for the liquor cabinet when they're experiencing writers' block. Douglas Adams famously took long baths and found that lying largely submerged in hot water was the best way to clear his mind and figure out where his hitchhikers should go next in their quest to explore the universe on less than thirty Altairian dollars a day.

I've never been so prescriptive in my unblocking process and generally embarked on whatever meaningless, mindless task needed doing that day that didn't involve writing. Cleaning the bathroom and vacuuming the living room were both popular choices. Or making soup. Anything so long as I wasn't sat staring at the computer. When I was younger I used to go jogging but the old knees complain now if I break into a trot, let alone a canter. It never seems to matter what I do to take my mind off the problem, to unleash my unconscious mind if you want to get all pretentious about it. The important thing is that you're not trying to write or to consciously think about what you're writing and to have pen and paper handy in case inspiration comes to when you're chopping an onion. I sometimes wonder if the Ancient Egyptian scribes never went out without a chisel tucked into their loin cloth on such occasions in spite of the inherent dangers involved.

I expect some people would use the memo record function on their phone. I prefer the old fashioned ways of the quill and papyrus, the pencil and paper, because one, I don't always carry my phone with me and two, I don't want it smelling of onions or garlic next time I phone someone after making some soup. Incidentally I like to think that Hamlet's famous soliloquy, "2b or not 2b" has for centuries been wrongly transcribed and is not about his own life and death, but his uncle's choice of pencil as murder weapon to drive into the old King's noggin. I'm assuming of course that Uncle Claudius didn't have any "slings and arrows" handy which surely would otherwise have done the job quite nicely.

I've always thought that pouring poison in the old King's ear was a most unlikely cause of death. Anything remotely resembling a "wet willy" in my ear would wake me up even after the heartiest meal. The Old King's ghost says he was sound asleep, "full of bread" in the orchard, which makes this perhaps the first recorded reference of someone suffering from a wheat intolerance and should be taken as an early promotion of a gluten free diet. It's also a precautionary tale about falling asleep in orchards unless you're Sir Isaac Newton and you're thinking is blocked and you're hoping for a flash of inspiration and a scientific breakthrough in the field of gravity. So there you have it, Hamlet's dad's demise was death by pencil or possibly a self inflicted wound, death by cotton bud, because he really couldn't stand listening to another five acts of his annoying, whiny, dithering son.

I'm fully aware that I am possibly guilty of hypocrisy here, being myself a world class ditherer. If indecision were an Olympic sport like soccer, me, Hamlet and Macbeth would be your back three. Perhaps that is the reason why I can't stand the Prince of Denmark. Listening to his endless what ifs and what ands is too likely *"to hold as 'twere the mirror up to nature."* Watching the play is like looking at my own reflection. And the biggest irony of all is that the mirror bit is his advice to the dodgy bunch of actors about to recreate his father's death in front of the court. Surely one of the worst choices in history for after dinner theatre.

So put off procrastination till tomorrow and have pencil and paper always at the ready since the flash of inspiration will always come when you're not consciously looking for it. As in this instance when I hadn't even realised that something was wrong with the play when I wrote it in the first place. I didn't know that something needed fixing, that the new ending would be so much more fun that the original one.

Sometimes like Douglas Adams I would be the happy recipient of these bolts from the blue, these flashes of inspiration, when I was in the bathroom. Only not in the bath since for one thing I didn't have one. I have a shower. Sometimes they did come to me in the shower but more often… I don't know how to put this without being indelicate. Sometimes they come to me when I'm in a sitting position.

Sorry, but sometimes that's where I make shit up, no pun intended. There I went ahead and got indelicate about it.

In my experience women are somewhat embarrassed by going to the toilet especially when it comes to number twos. That V.I.POO spray that I see advertised on TV is definitely marketed towards women, so that nobody need know what you were up to behind that closed door. Men, whether they admit it or not, are uniquely proud of this activity. Breaking wind comes in a close second. My father, for one, was never more amused than when he'd just let one rip. And let's be honest, everybody does both.

Women, nevertheless, are not so enamoured or intrigued by such activities. I think the two most significant indications are that a relationship is going somewhere are when someone says 'I love you' for the first time and when you are comfortable with cracking one off first thing in the morning like a bugler sounding '*Reveille*'.

Women also frown disapprovingly if you have a shelf of books in the toilet but come on, be reasonable. You might be in there some time and how else are you going to amuse yourself. How indeed? You can tell a lot about a man by what he reads on the toilet. It's like looking at someone's music collection back in the day when that was also displayed on a bookshelf and not concealed on a hard drive. Stuart liked to keep the most bizarre books that he came across remaindered in his bookshop. *Pig Diseases* won hands down in my opinion.

Famously men wonder what women talk about when they are alone and I'm pretty sure it's something more earthy than knitting and nail varnish. What men talk about among themselves to my certain knowledge (alright, Stuart) is their most recent toilet visit especially if they have just hoisted trou and emerged either triumphant or disconsolate from the smallest and now smelliest room in the house.

Stuart has in the past informed me that he has just spent fifteen minutes trying to expel a golf ball and on one occasion proudly announced that his most recent motion was positively symphonic in composition, that is in three distinct movements with different time signatures: *lento, andante and allegro*, with the brass and woodwind sections very much to the fore.

In short Stuart is always happy to inform anyone and anybody he passes with a newspaper tucked under his arm that he's "just off to the library."

Famously you never saw John Wayne or Jimmy Stewart in a Western nip off to spend a penny or go for a poo when they circled the wagons for the night, no matter how long they'd spent in the saddle that day. Makes you wonder how different history could have been if the Apaches had changed the habit of a lifetime and made a night attack. They could have caught the cowboys with their pants down and no mistake.

And don't tell me you didn't giggle when the actor, Burton Gilliam, let one rip in *Blazing Saddles*, the first fart to be featured in thunderous stereo in a movie theatre, gloriously followed by the next twenty-one farts to feature in film history. Yes, I counted them. Go on Youtube and try it for yourself. See what number you come up with. It will really improve your day. Incidentally there are also two burps. Never let it be said that Mel Brooks didn't do subtle.

Just not as subtle as Stanley Kubrick six years before. Maybe like me you recalled Mel's campfire scene with a sly, secret smile when you watched the sequence in *2001, a Space Odyssey* where precisely nothing happens for a minute or so while we observe one of the space travellers reading the instructions on how to use the zero gravity toilet. I like to call it Kubrick's silent fart scene.

So, yes I was sitting on the throne when I suddenly came up with a better ending for a play which Stuart and I might have put on several years before if only we'd had a bit of cash. And, yes, I did have to mute the mic when I let one rip like a schoolboy playing the trumpet while on the phone with Stuart because, even though he'd known where I was and what I was doing, nobody needs to hear that down the phone, do they? I think it's what they call telephone etiquette. And that's why I didn't have anything handy to write down what I'd come up with and I couldn't go and get a pencil and paper because the trumpet solo announced that I wasn't quite finished the mindless, meaningless task that had engaged my unconscious so delightfully and unexpectedly. What I did have was a mobile phone in my back pocket. Hence why Stuart was the lucky first to hear the good news and lucky for me we've been friends for a long time so he didn't put the phone down on me.

So whereas calling up my best friend from the toilet might not have been in the best taste, it was in the long term a sensible course of action to take if I didn't want my lucky flash of inspiration to disappear in a drunken, 'wait a minute I had a good idea yesterday, now what was it?' scenario. What was a less sensible and less forgivable course of action was what I did next, given that the Bloody Mary's were really kicking in and I was well and truly half cut. Maybe a little more than half.

Because what I did next was to call Faith.

"Hello, Faith, it's me."

"Who?"

"Me."

"Ben?"

"Yes, gentle Ben."

"Are you drunk?"

"That's entirely possible."

"Look, Ben, it's nice to hear from you but_"

"Listen, just listen a minute. Just a second. Shhhh. Just listen... I've got good news and bad news..."

"Give me the good news, I could do with some good news. But just be quick about it, will you?'

"The good news is that I won the lottery."

"That is good news. Did you win a lot?"

"Quite a bit. But that's not the really good news... The really good news is that I'm going to put on a play and you're going to be in it. Now who's your agent and are you available?"

"Yes, but… Ben, can you Facebook me and I'll give you my email address. You can send me the script."

"Okay. Now for the bad news. I have a confession to make. I had a huge crush on you at drama school. I think I was a teeny weeny bit in love with you_"

"Yes, I know, Ben. I think everyone knew and it's sweet of you to call but_"

"But in my defence I think everyone at drama school was a bit in love with you. Students, teachers, every man, woman, and child. You're a very loveable person, a very lovely, lovely person and I just want you to know that…"

"Look, I've got to go and pick up Jack from school. Ben, are you okay? Why is there an echo? You sound like you're in a church or something."

"Gotta go. My bum's beginning to stick to the… er…

"You're bum's doing what?"

"Never mind. Just look out for that message on Facebook"

Chapter Sixteen
The Grapes of Wrath

I have always lived violently, drunk hugely, eaten too much or not at all, slept around the clock or missed two nights of sleeping, worked too hard or too long in glory, or slowed for a time in utter laziness. I've lifted, pulled, chopped, climbed, made love with joy, and taken hangovers as a consequence, not as a punishment.

John Steinbeck, *Travels with Charley*.

Chapter Seventeen

Hangovers as both a punishment and a consequence…

Among the reasons I never made it to Oxford, apart from my working class hero pose were that I would have had to go back to school for another term in order to sit the entrance exam. This would also have meant another year studying the Classics; Latin, Greek, and Ancient History, which I'd taken for A' Levels on the advice of a teacher against my better judgement because it was a back door into Oxford and Cambridge and probably still is.

The numbers game is simply more in your favour as a Classics candidate than say English or Mathematics. Not a cake walk to get in but certainly an easier route for minds like mine that would not have been up to snuff otherwise. Boris Johnson got in that way and would have been a contemporary of mine had I gone. Need I say more? There but for the grace of God… Good God, I could have been Prime Minister…

The rationale behind my teacher's argument for studying the Classics against my will (Latin not too bad, Ancient History quite interesting, Ancient Greek absolutely ghastly and fiendishly difficult) was that once I'd got into Oxford by the back door I could then change to whatever subject or subjects I wanted to study. You can judge the wisdom of this strategy by the fact that I never went to Oxford and I can scarcely remember a word of Ancient Greek.

What I can remember are the bon mots and words of wisdom that my teacher liked to share that were either genuine pearls of ancient Athenian wisdom or simply ones that my teacher liked and had translated into Ancient Greek. Two of these, translated back into English, were "nothing in excess" and "I hate a fellow drinker who remembers what I said".

Both of these sayings seemed to be very appropriate to the hangover I was suffering as a consequence of, and punishment for, drinking too many Vegan Vogon Bloody Mary's the afternoon (and early evening) of the previous day until I'd either fallen asleep on the sofa or run out of vodka.

My prone position on the couch and the empty bottle of Stolichnaya on the floor next to me implied it might have been both. Proof if ever it was needed that drinking a more expensive variety of alcohol is no guarantee of a clear head the next day, but, hey, if you've just won the lottery you've got to treat yourself.

Apparently Russian vodka drinkers never propose a toast to future events, only those in the past like

'Here's to Stalin and the Great Patriotic War' or whatever. A night spent with a bottle of Moscow's finest hadn't left me inclined to drink a toast either to my recent past or my immediate future. Instead, I did what many modern drinkers do the next morning. I reached for my mobile phone to see who had been the unfortunate recipients of my drunk dialling the night before… Problem: no phone in sight.

 Moving very gingerly, I stood up to answer the morning call of nature heard by every man and dog since time began and in doing so found my phone. What was it doing in the bathroom?

My phone had gone into sleep mode on the official website for Stolichnaya, https://stoli.com, which informed me in case I had forgotten from the night before (I had) that Stolichnaya was now made from alcohol manufactured in Russia mixed with the purest spring water from Latvia before advising me to "savour Stoli responsibly" and to "drink with care". Two pieces of advice I'd clearly ignored the day before.

Dangerous stuff that Latvian spring water.

The recent calls list on my phone told me that I'd spoken to Stuart. That was no surprise.

The name Dai Young rang a vague bell in my head for some reason but who was he and why had I called him? No, there was no Dai Young in the recent calls list or in my contacts. Oh wait, the play… I was going to change the title of the play and rewrite the ending. Oh God.

I hate a fellow drinker who remembers what I said because…

Next on the list was a ninety second phone call to Faith… That didn't ring any bells at all. But how much trouble could I have got into in ninety seconds? Think, think hard. No… no recollection of speaking to Faith. None whatsoever. Probably just a pocket dial when I hoisted trousers after my phone call to Stuart. The time signatures on the recent calls list were pretty close together. That must be it. A pocket dial. The conversation with Stuart and the location from which it was made were beginning to come back to me in greater clarity and detail. My hindquarters were still feeling a little tender and with further examination in the bathroom mirror I thought I could still detect the ring of shame around my buttocks. Did I fall asleep on the toilet?

As a rule I've never been one of those people who wake up on the morning after who say "never again". Einstein's advice about repeating the same action expecting different results was making quite a bit of sense on the other hand. Nothing in excess. Apart from excess. No, that's what got you into trouble last night. Everything in moderation. Except moderation. Very clever. No, smart as in smarty pants but not clever.

Some people drink too much when they're sad and yes, I've drowned as many sorrows as the next man. But I also drink too much when I'm happy. Happy but alone as was the case last night when I'd had enough vodka to loosen both the bowels and the unconscious mind to come up with the new ending for the play. And had I not been alone I might have stopped midway through the bottle. But I was alone. Excited and alone. And I wanted to tell someone more about this great new ending for the play. Unfortunately my only companion after I'd called Stuart was seemingly Comrade Stolichnaya, who to be fair to him had been quite a good listener. His upturned emptiness on the floor bore witness to that.

Right, on with the day. I could hear my father's daily advice offered each and every morning when he knocked on my door to wake me up on a school day. "Another day dawneth full of promise and hope. Grasp the nettle firmly and it will sting thee not." I didn't really feel strong enough to grasp any nettles, firmly or otherwise. "I'll start work on the play tomorrow" I promised myself. Cross my heart and hope to be sober. Not really in the mood for beginning a rewrite and probably best to stay away from the computer in my current state of mind and slightly unsteady state of hand. That didn't sound like an excuse, more like sound advice. MacBooks don't come cheap, remember.

I'll maybe just write a quick note to Faith about the play. Find out if she's free. I always like to know who I'm writing for. It helps. Even if you don't know who's going to play the part it's helpful to cast it in your head. For example, I'll tell myself I'm writing this part for, say, a Tom Selleck type or a Woody Allen. As you can imagine the characterisation and dialogue and diction and speech patterns would be pretty different for both these actors if you've provisionally cast them in your imagination. Lots of writers do this. If you pick any kind of novel bought at an airport, say the kinds of thriller that get turned into movies like the Bourne trilogy, you can often tell from the description of the hero on page one of the book that the author's got Clint Eastwood in mind rather than Woody Allen.

This, of course, was the source of much hilarity when Tom Cruise played Lee Child's hero, Jack Reacher, who is blonde and six foot five in the books whereas Cruise is well, not. He couldn't Reacher Jack if he stood on a box. The one guy who's probably still laughing is the author because Cruise bought the movie rights to all seventeen books. Yes, sir, thank you, ma'am, laughing all the way to the bank.

So it would be good to know if Faith was free. Writing for someone small and free and full of bounce like Faith is completely different than writing for someone tall and languorous like a Rosamund Pike (five foot eight and a half and therefore significantly taller when playing opposite Jack-can't-quite-Reach-her Tom Cruise even if you believe that he's five foot seven. And it helps if you know the person but this works almost as well if you're pretend casting a movie star. Once you're a movie star with few exceptions you're type cast from the day you earn your first ten million dollar contract.

Oh wait. I don't think I've got an email address for her... Facebook. She's on Facebook. For once, a good reason for the existence of Facebook. And, as if by magic, there was a message from Faith on my phone sent an hour before on the dreaded F-book which read "Hi, Ben. Hope you're feeling better. Yes, I'd like to read your script when it's ready. My email address is… Faith475@…"

Oh good. Yes, I did call her but I didn't say anything stupid. Just told her about the play.

I don't have to worry about bumping into any of last night's fellow drinkers down the ἀγορά.

"Agora" I said out loud to myself or else to no one in particular. "The Ancient Greek for the market or meeting place. Fancy me remembering that. Gives us the word agoraphobic."

Which was how I was feeling, just a bit. Didn't really fancy meeting anyone at all just now. What I need are some scrambled eggs. Please, God, tell me I've got some eggs so I don't have to go down to the shop… or ἀγορά. Or a Bloody Mary. Hair of the dog… No, eggs. Scrambled eggs. Nothing in excess.

Chapter Eighteen

Another Day Dawneth…

Full of promise and hope. And no hangover. Time to grasp nettles firmly and get cracking on the rewrite. Faith liked the old script I sent her, so now I just had to find one more actor and change the ending. Full of hope, I sat down in front of my trusty Macbook.

Faith, hope and love but the greatest of these is…

It will be nice to see Faith again.

Will it? I hope so. Over her. Completely. One hundred per cent. She's married now. Got a kid. Two kids. And nobody ever sleeps with the writer. Who was the dumb blonde who was so dumb that she slept with the writer thinking it would help her get ahead in Hollywood. Who was that dumb blonde? Who was the writer? Was it Raymond Chandler?

"You gotta have faith…" Terrible song. Hate that song. Get out of my head.

"You gotta have Faith." Stop spelling faith with a capital F. That's all you need.

Concentrate, Ben. Get on with the rewrite. Don't worry about getting it right, get it written.

Re-written. God, this new ending's going to be great.

As I began re-working Act Three I began to realise how little I actually had to change of the play I had written, *Live Fast, Die Young* or to give it it's new title, *Live Fast, Dai Young*, in order to change my character's fate from suicide to murder by jealous ex-husband, played by Stuart. This climax was going to be so much snappier. It was bold, it was beautiful. And the new title meant I could lean on my favourite actor's crutch of putting on a funny voice or in this case a Welsh accent because all Welsh people sound funny so same thing really. Even the Bard of Avon thought so because surprisingly often he made a character Welsh for purely comic effect. Just the sound of a Welsh accent had them cracking up back in the 1600's which means Welsh people have sounded funny for centuries. All Welsh people with the sole exception of Richard Burton reading Dylan Thomas and slowly sinking in self importance under "the sloeblack, slow, black, crowblack, fishingboatbobbing sea."

The trick I've always found with writing is to hear the characters talking to you and sometimes I even see what they're doing on stage. It's as if you're not writing a play, you're watching it and hearing it. It's a play for voices like *Under Milk Wood* only it's in your head rather than on the radio. I wonder if that's how Dylan Thomas wrote. I'll bet it was. "I hold a beast, an angel and a madman within me". Sounds a bit like Stuart's character in the play. Don't think he'd be quoting Dylan Thomas though. Maybe Dai will. The heart and soul of a poet. Somebody once said that about me. That was a long time ago, wasn't it, boyo? "When one burns ones bridges, what a very nice fire it makes." That's Dylan Thomas too. Dylan Thomas and Robert Burns both poets, both died young, both lives ruined by drink. There's a pattern there. Here's to the candle that burns at both ends that will not last the night. But ah, my foes, and oh, my friends, it gives a lovely light. Slow fade into black.

Sloeblack, sloe gin, flavoured vodka, Stolichnaya, memo to self: don't buy, don't drink... "An alcoholic is someone you don't like who drinks as much as you do." Thank you Dylan, now shush. Concentrate, Ben. Control the voices. "To begin at the beginning..." of Act Three. You can do it, Dai, lovely boy...

I think it was Olivier or one of the greats who said he only found the character when he'd found the voice. "Now is the winter of our discontent made glorious summer" in that staccato, clipped delivery so roundly mocked by Peter Sellars. Was it spelt Sellars or Sellers? Anyway he took the piss out of Olivier doing Richard III. Yes, the old ham actor's trick of putting on a funny voice or giving the character a limp. You could do both of course if you were playing Richard. But hang on. I did still have a slight limp after my recent near miss with the double decker bus but it wasn't going to be me putting on the funny voice. I wasn't going to be playing the character of Dai. Just writing and directing. Probably just as well. Might start falling in love with Faith all over again and anyway she could always act me off the stage. Better tell Stuart to look to his game. I don't think he ever saw Faith act onstage. We were only in that one play at drama school, me and Faith. Weren't even onstage at the same time what with my character being dead by the time Act Three came around and Faith took on the role of Lu Ann.

Yes, the only time we acted together was in that awful improvisation which ended with me not knowing what to say to Lu Ann, to Faith. Blah blah blah, hate improv, this is torture, until I ran out of words and kissed her. And it was a pretty rubbish kiss and she didn't kiss back, Lu Ann or Faith. Wait, that might be a good scene though for Faith and Stuart. He begs her not to leave him for Dai and in desperation he kisses her. But she doesn't kiss back. I like that. Think I can use that. I liked the sound of that more and more the more I thought about it.

Some people liked my plays, some didn't. "Puerile, offensive rubbish" was the verdict of one literary manager when I pressed her to tell me what she honestly thought. Since she didn't think very much about the play and the thoughts she did think weren't very nice she'd been most reluctant to tell me in the first instance what she thought. I think she made the mistake of thinking I cared what she thought. I didn't. I was just curious. Her initial reticence had told me right away that 'masterful' was not likely to be one of her thoughts on what she'd read. What annoyed me was that she couldn't or wouldn't tell me why she didn't like it beyond some vague implication thats she found the characters unlikeable. If you want likeable go read Peppa Pig, who incidentally I find thoroughly unloveable and unpalatable in any form other than a sandwich.

They're mostly academics, the people who work for literary departments in theatres and their main task is finding a reason to say no to your scripts. Can't blame them entirely. They get so many unsolicited manuscripts these days. For non-luvvies or non-theatre folk an unsolicited script means the theatre hasn't commissioned the play. They haven't asked anyone to write it, let alone paid for them to write it. Someone like me has sent it to them unbidden in the only month in the year where the literary department or temporary hirelings thereof will actually read all these plays they don't really want to read. They call it a "script window". Out of which window your script will probably go, straight into the dumpster.

When I started writing plays you didn't have to get your script passed the growling jaws of a literary manager, sat like Cerberus at the front door of the theatre waiting for the postman to pop your masterpiece through the letter box. What you did back then was to write your play and send a nice professional letter to the Artistic Director with a synopsis of the script. And sometimes they said "yes, please, do send" and sometimes they said "no thanks, not for us, not our sort of material but have you thought of sending it to so-and-so?"

It was all so much more civilised and naturally I preferred it. My plays, you could like them or loathe them, but actors and directors, especially if they started out as actors, generally recognise good dialogue when they see it. Literary managers, not so much. They've never been actors. And if nothing else I wrote decent dialogue which all actors enjoy speaking. Perhaps I wrote a sort of downmarket, poor man's bargain basement *Hamlet.* Some nice lines, shame about the play.

Stuart liked to describe my dialogue as "sparkling, luv, sparkling" which was about the only time he ever used the term sparkling without adding "white wine for the lady at the end of the bar". And when he was talking about one of my plays was pretty much the only time Stuart was likely to pay me a genuine compliment. It's a guy thing.

So nice dialogue, shame about the plot. Plot and storyline, they were the absolute buggers I found, which was why I'd got the ending of this play wrong and was now rewriting it. The trick for me was not to worry too much about whether you knew where you were going. That and never to be afraid to get on the wrong bus, as it were. You could always go back to the bus stop and get on a different one. So while it was comforting to have a route map when I was writing, to have a rough idea of where I was going, I was never entirely sure it was the right map or the right destination and I didn't really care at the precise moment I hopped on any particular bus. The trick was to keep going till the following junction and see if you were excited about any of the destinations on the next road sign. It very seldom said "Dead End" or "No Through Road".

Sometimes this meant that the eventual destination might only be reached by a rather circuitous route or a complete re-write of act three. The trick was to be open to all possibilities, all bus routes as you were going along. I've lost count of the times the direction of a play or something a character has said has taken me by surprise and they're often the best bits, far better than anything I'd have come up with myself if I'd stuck closely to an outline.

The trick was to keep a light hold of the reins and give the horse it's head now and then. Let it go where it wants to go even if there's always the chance of it unseating you when it unexpectedly jumps over a hedge into a different field. Forgive me if I'm mixing my transport metaphors here but sometimes a horse can go where a bus can't. And sometimes you can sit back on the top deck of a tour bus and enjoy the view stretching for miles around and sometimes it's more like riding in the Grand National at Aintree and all you can see is the arse of the horse in front of you. But, if you hold on, the finish line will eventually come into view.

That's what writing's like. At least it is for me.

The play like everything else I'd ever written was part autobiography, part fantasy. In this case Stuart's character was called Stuart and mine had been called Ben because I'm deeply unimaginative when it comes to picking names. But I had no idea who was going to play the character which had been based on me. So I was still writing for "me" albeit in a Welsh accent for a character now called Dai because it gave me a title

that screamed dark COMEDY in the same way that
Les Miserables screams MISERY.

The plot, darling, you were going to tell us the plot.
That might help. Both male characters were in love
with the same woman and in the original version
she'd got married to Stu who was both taller and
better looking than Ben (Dai) and always got the girl.
Write what you know… And in the original version
she had left Stuart because he was a bit of a sleaze
bag (write what you know) and briefly taken me as a
lover before going back to Stuart, hence my
character's suicide.

The funny thing that was now dawning on me as I
wrote the new version is that this was more true to
real life than I realised. In real life real-life-Ben, i.e.
me, almost never got the girl he (I) was after. And
looking back there was an alarming number of one
night stands, fully consummated or otherwise, with
girls who were pissed off with their current
boyfriends to whose loving or cheating embrace they
duly returned the next day. Which might have been
part of their plan all along. They never told me and I
never asked. Perhaps I just assumed. When a girl tells
you she's got a boyfriend while she's taking her top
off there are a number of things you can assume are
going to happen next, God willing, but leaving said
boyfriend and shacking up with you is not necessarily
a safe assumption.

And looking back while re-writing the play it
occurred to me that this had happened a surprisingly
large number of times. Not dozens but enough to look

like a pattern. My sexual history was unfolding before me while I wrote. The aforementioned one night stands also bore an alarming resemblance to my nights comforting Fiona with the exception that with Fiona there was never a chance of me getting to third base or hitting the occasional home run. Occasional because in these, girl-on-a-twelve-hour-break-from-her-arsehole-boyfriend nights, I didn't always strike it clean out the park or over the fence. In baseball and bedroom parlance I was usually lucky if I rounded second base and flopped onto third. Never much of a lover or a fighter, me. But every dog has his day and so does every lover. Occasionally.

On the few occasions when I found myself with a girl who wasn't already in a relationship with someone else it ended with me thinking she was the wrong girl for me (she usually was) or an irritating change of circumstances got in the way as with me and Marie, *la belle flic* in France. I sometimes wondered if there was an invisible barcode on my forehead that only stray dogs and crazy women could read and I'd made the mistake of opening my door to more than my fair share of both.

Her "cheatin' heart will make you weep". Thanks for the warning, Hank. That's good advice but I'd never taken it yet.

The first step to changing a pattern as Albert Einstein might or might not tell you is spotting that there is one and correctly identifying the cause and effect in the sequence of events. Like drinking too much

Latvian spring water and having a hangover the next day.

Maybe it was having a bit more *chutzpah*, *moxie* or good old fashioned *cojones* after my lottery win that I was writing a scenario where the girl actually left the schmuck she was with and chose to be with me, with Dai. If you write it, she will come. It had a nice ring to it if nothing else. If I could conceive of it on the page maybe I could believe in it or bring it about in real life.

Of course there's a limit to the number of spots a leopard can change in one go which is perhaps why I couldn't quite bring myself to write the Hollywood romcom happy ending. No, Stuart was going to have to kill me in a jealous rage by popping a cap in my ass or rather in my head at point blank range so that it looked like suicide and he could get the girl back and give the eulogy I was about to write for the end of the play which I hoped might be actually quite moving in an ironic sort of way. Tears might be shed I even dared to hope.

Oh wait a mo. Hold the front page. I could open the play with Stuart's eulogy so that from the start the audience will be expecting Dai to commit suicide and whole play is in flashback leading up to that point and ends with a reprise of the start of Stuart's eulogy for dead Dai, now murdered Dai not suicidally depressed Dai.

Super ironic. Take that, Hollywood rom com ending! Funny how these ideas come to you just so long as you don't actively go looking for them.

So writing plays for me had always been mostly a case of letting my imagination run riot. It was about as much fun as I ever had with my clothes on. Or off. Ian… Ian Edwards. But Ian with the funny Welsh spelling. Faith's old boyfriend from drama school. That's who should play me. Wonder if he's available? Time to call his agent.

Chapter Nineteen
Wrong number.

So I had the beginning and the very end of the script in hand though not written and the casting was all in place assuming everyone was available. I knew Stuart was and Faith had more or less committed to doing it. That just left Ian and his agent had agreed to forward the original script. Momentum is important when you're writing, not because you've got to take advantage of when the Muse is upon your shoulder or some such bollocks. It's because speed of writing translates into energy on the page and hopefully from there onto the stage.

Drama, good drama is about action. By action I don't mean Vin Diesel, Schwarzenegger kind of action. It means the actors must be trying to do something to each other. A common trick with actors working on a script is to put active verbs in front of every line like "seduce" or "poke" or "annoy" to help them work out their motivation. Every character should want something from the other character, to be trying to do something to them, all the time. They might appear to be talking about the corn flakes they had for breakfast but what they're actually "saying" is I'm sick of this marriage and for your information I hate bloody corn flakes so why do you keep buying them? I want out and I want out now and I want sugar puffs, damn it.

Show, don't tell is one of the mantras you hear in theatre all the time. Bad drama is a couple of people just telling each other how they feel all the time. Soap operas are like that. People don't go around telling each other how they feel about everything unless they've done a lot of other things first.

The only exception to this rule is in sports interviews. The big centre forward telling the sports reporter how he felt when he scored the winner against Manchester United. "It's a great feeling but I'm just happy to be one of the lads. It was a team effort really." Why do journalists always ask how it felt. Honestly how do you think he felt? "Well, Brian, I hit the ball first time and there it was in the back of the net." John Cleese wrote that sketch fifty years ago but sports reporters are still asking how did it feel when…"

"It felt like a ball on the top of my boot, what do you think?" Or "I was looking at some fit bird in the crowd when the ball hit me smack in the face and it bloody well hurt".

Most people spend most of their lives hiding what they really feel from other people and from themselves. The only other exception to this rule that I can think of is my sister Kaye. She can't stop telling you how she feels about everything. She labours under the permanent delusion that you're someone who cares.

One famous playwright said that speaking should be a character's last resort, not the first. They were probably exaggerating for effect and the effect that I think they were going for is I'm a famous playwright and therefore entitled to be pretentious. But I know what they meant.

Sometimes when I start writing a scene I have just a couple of lines jotted down but they're usually key bits of dialogue that unlock the characters' motivation in the scene. Often I have no idea what the characters are going to say which is a lot of fun because you can be genuinely surprised by what they do say. You may not believe it but I've sometimes laughed out loud at what one of my characters comes out with. I've even on one occasion been moved to tears by a character in one of my scripts reading aloud the words of a suicide note I was writing. This was slightly embarrassing as I was sitting in Caffè Nero at the time. Maybe everyone thought I was crying about how much my coffee had cost in a Caffè where the second 'f' must surely stand for "fuck me, that's a lot to pay for a cup of coffee".

Often I will start writing a scene with just an idea of what a character's motivation is, what they're trying to do to one another or to get from each other. And then it's a race to get the words on the page. It's like a sprint to the finish line. This was where I was in the scene I was writing, a pivotal moment in the play between Stuart and Faith's characters. She was plucking up the courage to say she was leaving him. The marriage was over.

And then the worst thing that can happen at these times happened, when everything is flowing, when the scene is rolling down the hill to an inevitable climax like an avalanche of snow that will send your

112

characters tumbling or bury them in inarticulate fury. What happened was the telephone rang.

Your immediate reaction is to ask yourself why you never learn, why didn't you switch it off or take it off the hook like you could in the old days before cell phones. This doesn't work of course because now they send an annoying buzzing noise down the phone line to tell you that it's off the hook and that's against the rules because you've got to be reachable at all times. It's the law! And you think it will stop ringing if you just ignore it but it doesn't or worse still it stops then rings again so in the end you do what you always do and almost always regret doing. You pick up the phone and say "hello".

Now what you want to say is "I can't talk now I'm snowed under" or "there's an avalanche heading this way" or "you've got the wrong number, this is the dry cleaners" or "no, I don't have PPI" or just "fuck off, I'm working". None of these would have done the job on this occasion because the person on the end of the line was either not going to take the hint or was going to take offence.

It was my sister, Kaye.

Now I don't get many phone calls, least of all from my family. I haven't spoken to my brother in five years because he really is an alcoholic and the worst kind at that. He's the kind who can't admit they drink too much as opposed to me who knows he drinks too much and is pretty happy to admit it to anyone who asks unless you're my doctor. I refuse to discuss my drinking habits with anyone who is likely to use the phrase "units of alcohol". Stuart told me once that my brother was a dead ringer for Steve Coogan's comic alter ego, Alan Partridge, and though I'd never thought about it before he was dead right. My brother looks just like him and talks like him too. How do you know my brother is talking crap? His lips are moving. So imagine Alan Partridge drunk and very possibly armed and dangerous and ask yourself if this is the sort of person you want to spend time with. He once held a large kitchen knife to my throat. That made for memorable Christmas morning.

My other sister, not Kaye, the middle one, is simply one of the dullest human beings I know. She's the sort of person who keeps a very clean house and by clean I mean it looks like a show home. My middle sister, so dull I won't name her once, let alone twice, who could make a weekend in New York sound dull, was happily married for eighteen years with two kids until she decided she wasn't.

She spent the next eight years after the divorce regretting it. She found out being married to a really nice guy was not the worst fate that could befall you. The subsequent four boyfriends were. Some couples like Richard Burton and Elizabeth Taylor get divorced and think better of it, so they go back to give it another go. I've actually got a lot of respect for that. My sister on the other hand is the sort who thinks she hasn't made a mistake in the last twenty years and frankly I'm tired of hearing it.

The nearest she ever came to self-knowledge was to admit that her favourite song was an old Marianne

114

Faithful hit and like Lucy Jordan 'she could clean the house for hours or rearrange the flowers' and would 'never ride through Paris in a sports car with the warm wind in her hair.'

Neither she nor my brother are on my Christmas card list (I don't actually have one) and neither were invited to my birthday party or even know where I live. Come to think of it Kaye wasn't invited either but she came anyway. That's one of the drawbacks if you don't like your birthday and don't like your family and you were born on April 1st. It's one of those dates people don't forget.

Whereas my middle sister lives in perpetual denial that she is unhappy, Kaye is in a perpetual state of unhappiness and everyone else is to blame for it. Or maybe that's just the way she feels when she calls me. She's even unhappy about her name. She can't seem to decide whether she wants to be called Kate or Kathleen or… Kaye is the latest. Some women change their hairstyle when they're unhappy. Kate, or Kathleen, or Kaye changes her name.

I don't speak to Kaye often but I do at least speak to her. It doesn't usually take me long before I regret this. About ten minutes is average in person much less than that on the phone. I suppose there are a lot of people who only phone you when they want something from you and Kaye is one of these. Annoyingly what she often wants or appears to want is your opinion on whatever harebrained scheme she has come up with. She doesn't really want your opinion. She wants to hear that you agree with what she thinks.

Her latest wheeze is to become a writer and yes, my heart sank because I knew she would call me more often than before to ask my opinion. Put it in an email are not words Kaye understands. I know I should on no account tell her what I think and should keep my opinion to myself since I know or at least suspect that anything she writes is the sort of thing that only a therapist should read. And he's being paid to read it. I'm not.

Memo to self: I really must get caller display on this landline.

What was particularly worrying about this particular phone call was that I couldn't figure out why she was calling right now other than vague enquiries about my well being, the more specific enquiries being was I worried about the possibility of my impending death and had I decided what to do with the money.

My specific answers, specific but not entirely truthful, were fine, no, and no. I knew exactly what I was going to do with some of the money, put on a play, and I was slightly concerned still about possibility of dying unexpectedly. Concerned but not out and out afraid. But I wasn't about to tell that to Kaye. Painful experience had told me that anything you said to her was liable to come back to haunt you from her mouth, sometimes years later, in a vaguely recognisable but twisted form. She had peripheral memory. Not quite accurate and just off to the wrong side of insanity.

What was a cause of real concern was that the real reason behind my sister's phone call remained a mystery at the end of an unusually short phone conversation with her. Normally with Kaye you could put the phone down and make a cup of tea, come back and say "uhuh" and she was none the wiser and no further forward. But this little chat was short. Very short. It was time to be afraid. Very afraid.

No, forget about that for now. Time to get back to the script.

What is wrong with this new word processor? Why can't I get the formatting right?

Chapter Twenty

Memento Mori

Centre stage is a coffin with something resembling a BAFTA Award on top of it. Downstage right there is a microphone on a microphone stand.

Stuart

This is very strange, I've never played a church before, so it's good to see so many familiar faces here. I can even see a few friendly ones.

Thinking about what I should say here today, I must confess that my first reaction was to panic – 'What can I say about Dai Morgan?' I thought. Because Dai Morgan was …an arsehole. A grumpy, surly, cantankerous, short-arsed, self-obsessed arsehole. And those were just his good points. Who but an arsehole would blow his brains out in his bathroom when he'd just had new tiles put in? And what a mess he left behind him. Close friends, a sparkling career as the second funniest man from Swansea, and a

lot of unpaid bills. Why? I don't
know why. Maybe he changed his
mind about the tiles. Maybe he just
wanted to piss us off. Yes, Dai
Morgan was an arsehole alright, but
I think I can speak for everyone
here when I say that Dai was my
very favourite arsehole.

He was the brother I never had. He
made boarding school bearable. He
even introduced me to Judy, my
wife. He was the best man at my
wedding, the godfather of my eldest
son and he was late on both
occasions. I suppose from now on
he'll always be late. And, of course,
he was my comedy partner for the
last ten years. We were always a
double act, right from the start, but
'Take Two' will be no more. From
now on it'll just be 'Take'.

We lived most of our lives in each
other's pockets. And anyone who
ever met Dai would know that his
pockets were not a very nice place
to be. They were generally full of
scraps of paper. Jokes and one
liners, ideas for sketches or a new
show, and, of course, his final piece

of work, a short and decidedly unfunny suicide note, typed on the back of his unfinished novel, a note that left us wondering "how did this happen?' and 'why was his spelling so bad?'

Dai carried his life around in his pockets. You could usually find his lunch in there too. Going through his pockets that day, I found the name and number of every person Dai cared about. That and an uneaten Danish pastry. Yes, Dai's pockets are the reason that all of you are here today. You were all in there.

I feel very privileged to be here with you all, because I wasn't in there. My number wasn't in Dai's pocket. That makes me feel very special indeed. Dai Morgan knew what my number was ... Yes, in the end he knew what my number was.

Words are so inadequate on these occasions, so I'd like to finish by playing this song because, well, because Dai simply hated it, and this'll really piss him off.

SX. Organ plays 'Happy Birthday'. Stuart exits. Music cross fades into canned laughter followed by applause.

Female V.O.   And this year's Best Newcomer in television comedy is … if I can get into this envelope …[*SX. A little laughter*] … the award goes to… Stuart McGill and Dai Morgan for *The University of Life.*

[SX. *Applause and cheering overlap the Male Voice Over below.*]

Male V.O.   Channel 4's *The University of Life,* written by Dai Morgan and starring Dai Morgan and Stuart McGill was one of the unexpected hits of 1996, and promises a great future for this talented young comedy duo.

During the Male Voice Over Dai steps onto the stage from where he has been sitting in the audience as if at an awards ceremony. He picks up the award from on top of the coffin and moves to the microphone as SX. applause fades.

Dai   I'd like to thank everyone who
             voted for *The University of Life* as
             best new comedy of 1996. I'm sorry
             that Stuart couldn't be here tonight.
             He's off on some beach on his
             honeymoon at the moment. So if
             you're watching, "Hello Stu... Hi
             Judy... Missing you already..."
             Ernest Hemingway once said "a
             writer must write what he has to
             say, not say it", so I'll shut up now.
             But please keep watching...

PART TWO

Chapter Twenty-One

A Play on Words

Reasonably pleased with that opening for the play.
Probably run it by Stuart though if he suggests
specific changes they're usually facetious and a bit
picky. He has this thing about wanting his lines to be
grammatically correct whereas I keep telling him it's
dialogue. Nobody speaks grammatically in real life
so... Of course, if you wrote dialogue that actually
resembled real speech it would include all sorts of
um's and er's and repetitions and be either completely
pretentious or tedious or er... you know... like
both... tedious and pretentious.

But apart from that he's got basically sound instincts
about a script so I listen to what he has to say. This
isn't always true for actors in general or their agents.
If you're wondering why you sometimes see famous
actors in lousy films that might be why. Some of them
can't tell a good script from a bad one. Either that or
they needed the money. And as for some agents, well,
they're just greedy. They always want the money.
Another thing about actors that's not generally known
is that they're not that bright as a rule. Emotionally
intelligent maybe, but academically? Not so much.
Surprisingly few of them have been to university. A
gross generalisation, it's true, but like most
generalisations generally true. When you get down to

it most of them don't have a Scooby-Doo when it comes to Shakespeare. Do they have a clue what he's saying? They Scooby-Don't.

Unfortunately this means that some actors rely heavily on directors who, spoiler alert, gross generalisation coming, generally have gone to university but have the emotional intelligence of a two year old. They mostly have no idea when it comes to getting into the heart of a character, having spent their university years in the library unlike me in The Stag's Head. Most of them for instance would not know that in Scooby-Doo, Shaggy's real name is Norville. Now most directors would insist you search your soul, your emotional memory for why a character would be scared of his own shadow and comfort eat their way through an endless supply on Scooby Snacks but all you really need to know if you're playing a character like Shaggy is that his real name is Norville.

All the best directors that I've worked with have one thing in common. They say surprisingly little in rehearsal. The bad ones never shut up. A good director will have the patience to let an actor make his own journey in his own time, maybe with a gentle prompt here and there, always encouraging, never saying no, least of all to love. It's a nurturing process at best. Or to cut the crap, a good director knows when and where to throw on a little manure to help their flowers blossom. Too much talk from a director, too much manure, and all you're left with is a load of manure. Bullshit in other words.

Any good director, and the good ones are fairly modest in my experience, will tell you that if you have a decent script and you get the casting right you're almost home. Job done. Almost.

With Stuart I pretty much knew what I was going to get. He's a bit of a refrigerator actor like myself and he tends to give pretty much the same performance every time but every now and then a little but of magic happens almost in spite of him. In a completely different way I was pretty sure what to expect from Faith. Faith is almost the complete opposite of Stuart as an actor, completely natural, seemingly effortless, artless even.

Ars est celare artem. That's your actual Latin and therefore something that Faith would never have heard of let alone understand but by God she could do it. Her skill as an artist, entirely untaught because perhaps the real artists don't need to be taught, was in concealing the art.

So the director, yours truly in this case, was pretty happy with the script (lucky that because he was the one what wrote it) with it's new beginning and ending and he had more or less complete confidence in two thirds of his cast.

Now we just had to hope that Ian was an Olivier sort of actor. That is once he'd found the right voice, and Ian was from Swansea so he had the voice, once he'd found the voice he'd found the character.

What could possibly go wrong?

Chapter Twenty-Two
Playing Games

Live Fast, Dai Young: Rehearsal Diary
Day 1: 10.00. Fun and Games.

        10.30. Table read through and discussion.

        13.00. Lunch.

        14.00 Second table read through.

        16.00 Questions arising from second read through.

        17.00 Further business.

        18.00 Pub.

Chapter Twenty-Three

Play Up

Rehearsing a play can take shape in many different forms or formats, there being no hard and fast rule about what's the best way to go about it and especially how to begin. The material, that is the script, is probably the biggest deciding factor and next comes the director. How do they like to work. Before play comes the foreplay. Fun and games. Almost always you start with a few icebreakers but how to proceed after that? There are lots of different ways to skin the cat in order to get down to the bare bones. Some theatre folk like to describe the rehearsal process as peeling the layers off an onion but the more you think about that metaphor the more likely tears will result as all you get when you peel back the layers of an onion is more layers of onion.

We started in this case to play ball by playing with balls. A few simple ball games to break the ice and to kill a little time waiting for Ian who'd texted to say he'd be late which is what he was. Twenty minutes but who's counting? It was not a good start.

Table read through and discussion needs no further explanation other than the distinction that you're reading the script for the first time sitting round a table rather than "getting it on its feet" which comes later, perhaps first blocking the actors moves onstage if you're an old fashioned sort of director.

Some actors give what is uncannily like a radio play or audio version of what will be their final performance which makes you wonder why you're bothering to pay for a cold, dusty church hall with a leaky roof as a rehearsal space. Stuart's one of these and I probably plead guilty on that score too. It's one of the curses I think of actors who have been to university and are reasonably literate by nature. They're perhaps more head than heart.

Faith's not one of these. She can read, of course, but she's not especially literate in the academic sense. I was confident, however, that once we got on our feet she was going to make the rest of us look like amateurs. Ian, well, Ian gave me the strong impression that this was the first time he'd actually looked at the script.

Bugger. This wasn't going well. This Ian thing might not work out.

Discussion. Faith didn't contribute much but that didn't surprise. She's not really one to talk things out. More a seat of the pants type. And Stuart's read this play or one very much like it once before with the only difference this time being that in this version he's a low down, cheating bastard who's capable of murder instead of a just low down bastard who cheats on his wife.

So that just left....

"I don't get it."

"What don't you get, Ian? Sorry, is it Ian or how is it pronounced? I know it's not spelt…"

"It's spelt I-e-u-a-n but people always say it wrong so I tell everyone at the start of rehearsals just to call me Ian."

"Got it. Now what is it that you don't… get? You've got the accent down something lovely by the way" I said, attempting a Welsh accent and immediately regretting it. The Welsh accent can be a bit of a bugger if you haven't practised it and can easily come out not so much Newport as New Delhi.

"I'm from Swansea, so of course I can do the accent."

"So what's the problem with the play?" asked Stuart, just about concealing the fact that he wasn't feeling immediately warm and fuzzy towards Ieuan either.

"I just don't get… okay, for a start I don't get why Judy doesn't go for Dai, why does she go for Stuart?"

"Sex appeal, charm, what's not to like?" Stuart said.

"He's a total bastard."

"Women don't always go for the nice guy."

Which was precisely what I was going to say only Faith got there first. Which surprised me, first that she wanted to take part in the discussion, which was heading dangerously towards an argument and second because there was something about the way she said it. Past history, bad boyfriend, I supposed. Present company not excluded.

"Okay here's another thing" Ieuan continued. "Why doesn't Dai tell her how he feels about her. He's obviously in love with her from the start."

"I can think of a number of reasons but I think that's something you need to think about for yourself because it's you who's playing Dai not me. Why don't we break for lunch? Back at two if that's alright with everyone?"

"I have to go at three. I've got an audition at four-thirty."

How odd you didn't mention it before, I thought, which was worrying but what was more worrying was that I wasn't sure I cared.

"Actually it would suit me to finish early too." Faith said. "My mum's having to pick Jack up from school for me so…"

"Okay, its just the first day" I said, "but in future…"

"In future" Stuart said "we'll tell you ahead of time if there's any scheduling problems."

"Thanks, I'd appreciate that. Good luck with the audition. What's it for?"

"Telly."

"Nice. Hope you get it." And I found myself really hoping he got it. We'd started off the rehearsal playing games and I had a nasty feeling that we'd ended up with some game playing.

Memo to self: we might need to find another actor. And a stage manager. So I didn't have to keep a bloody rehearsal diary.

Live Fast, Dai Young: Rehearsal Diary (amended)
Day 1   1800 Trip to pub: cancelled due to lack of interest.

Chapter Twenty-Four

Pay or Play

Unaccustomed as I am with working with money and unaccustomed as I was to having any money to speak of, my previous theatre productions, if that's not too pretentious a term, did not function on a particularly professional basis in terms of organisation. Or finance.

What sort of organisation do you need when the whole "production" was mostly thrown together by you and your flatmate in the confines of your own home. Written, costumed, designed and often rehearsed in your front room. Budget? What budget? Lighting by electricity, special effects by accident. This was the world of "profit share" theatre and if I was not altogether happy working in this wain the past I was at least familiar with it. If you're lucky enough to be working in film or television things are quite different. To give you an example right off the top of my head an actor might be engaged to work on an upcoming film production on a "pay or play" contract. Sounds a bit confusing and it's name, while snappy, doesn't to my mind accurately describe what it represents. What it boils down to is this. You, the actor have been provisionally cast in a movie. Lucky you. And you're going to be paid. Whoopee!

Now for the sneaky bit. You can be fired or removed from the project for pretty much any reason whatsoever with little or no legal comeback. But you still get paid even if the director decides he doesn't like you or finds out you're difficult to work with or thinks your an arse with a silly Welsh name that's just downright difficult to spell.

Do you see where I'm going with this?

I don't know about you but I've never fired anybody. So I was feeling a little nervous about this since actors are emotional beings and nobody wants to hurt someone else's feelings unless you're Sir Alan Sugar or Donald Trump and you treat hiring and firing the sorcerer's apprentice in the same easy and casual manner.

Also this particular emotional being whom I was considering firing was not so very little. Built like a rugby player and prone towards the passive aggressive as I'd discovered the day before. Now as a rule I don't do conflict. To be more precise I don't do conflict well so I was a little apprehensive. I was more than a little concerned about the possibility of aggression building to the active side of passive. If I was going to do it I wanted to do it in a professional manner.

I certainly wasn't going to do it in some crass way like sending a text.

Which was I felt a somewhat lucky coincidence because that's how Ieuan announced he was quitting and had broken the news to Faith just as she came into our rehearsal space. The gist of the text was that he didn't want to be a part of this project and anyway he was now in line for a recurring role in a new soap opera on the Welsh speaking channel, S4C.

That's at least the gist of it that we got second hand from Faith reading off her phone.

"He might have said 'sorry'" said Stuart

"I guess he's probably not sorry. Can't really blame him for doing telly," I said.

Truth was I didn't really care. Thinking about how to nip the Ieuan thing in the bud before it got out of hand had kept me awake the night before but not long enough to come up with a solution to the obvious problem that now presented itself.

"So who's going to play Dai?" asked Stuart.

I can't say for sure that a rhetorical question was implied but something about Stuart's attitude and the fact that his gaze was fixed on me suggested to me that he wasn't so much asking me who should play Dai as telling me.

"Oh no, no, no, no."

I hoped that would be the end of it but Stuart came right back at me.

"Why not? It seems like the obvious solution. You originally wrote the part for yourself."

"Not now it's Welsh... Written for a Welsh actor."

"You love doing a Welsh accent. And I'm sure in time, with a little practice, you'll sound a bit more like Anthony Hopkins and less like someone taking a telephone order for two orders of chicken tikka with chapatis and pilau rice."

"I don't want to direct and act at the same time. It won't work."

"It worked before."

"That was just you and me. Just the two of us. It wouldn't be fair to Faith."

"I don't mind giving it a try," said Faith. "Someone's got to at least read the lines until we find another actor to play Dai."

Now ever since I'd first seen Faith act I was pretty much disinclined to say no to any suggestion she might have made. In this case the logic of her argument was inescapable.

"Okay," I said. "Since this is kind of unexpected and I'm pretty much unprepared, what do we say to starting afresh tomorrow with another read through?"

"You're cancelling the day's rehearsal? On the second day of rehearsal?" said Stuart.

"Seeing as how it's going so tremendously well I thought you all deserve to take a day off."

So that's what we did.

Chapter Twenty-Five

Playing Along

Rehearsal Day Two, or was it Three, finished and back home in my digs that with my newly acquired wealth were feeling increasingly dingy, I poured myself a measure of Glenmorangie.

Alright, more like a measure and a half.

My resolution to quit drinking, or at least drinking alone, for the duration of rehearsals had not really got past even the conceptual stage. I could however, remember a stage in my life when I still nurtured hopes for a successful career on the stage where I drank a good deal less than now. And back then my landlady, Sarah, a lawyer and sometimes Brixton housemate, used to celebrate every lowly acting job I got by taking me out to the local rum bar. I think it's a cafe now that Brixton has become gentrified but back then it was a tiny rum bar with an enviable array of bottles of sugar cane derived spirits imported from the islands.

Their best selling cocktail was called a Brixton Riot and how could you not order a drink with a name like that. Suffice to say that rioting was the last thing on your mind after drinking one of these. You heard the call of the hammock and the shade of a palm tree if you could in fact find anything so exotic in Brixton back then.

And if ever I got a *salaried* job in the theatre I celebrated by treating myself to a bottle of malt whisky and back then it would last me a good deal longer than now in more sodden times. But I'd bought a bottle of Glenmorangie now in the theory that a better class of liquor might encourage me to sip rather than gulp.

Well, it was a theory. Of sorts.

If you're into toponymy, that's the meaning or study of place names to thee and me, Glenmorangie means Glen of Tranquility. Come to think of it, I think there used to be an advert on telly that said much the same thing.

And tranquility was what I sought.

So I lay there on the couch going back over my recent emotions recollected in tranquility. Seeing Faith again had been okay. Surprisingly okay.

Okay… there's a description of emotion that Wordsworth would have been proud of.

Okay… so he'd have been anything but okay with that description but not being much of a romantic or a poet I was pretty okay with okay.

It was much better than what I used to feel like talking to Faith. Tongue tied. Emotionally bound and conversationally useless.

Okay was definitely an improvement. So maybe rehearsing with her would be… just fine this time. Not weird at all.

So that was good and long may it continue. Probably helps that she's married now. And a mother. Two kids. Little Faith all grown up and obviously better off without that arsehole Ian whichever way you spelt it. I didn't remember him being such an arse at drama school but, wait… feeling less tranquil now. Change the subject. Enough of the past, let's deal with the present and the immediate future.

One more shot of Glenmo' then put the bottle out of reach of children and me in the kitchen cupboard. All too easy to reach for it when it's on the coffee table. No need to get riotous.

Ping! A text from Faith. Momentary heart flutter when I see it's from her. Luckily the content was nothing to be overly concerned about. It seemed she'd found us a stage manager. Someone who was on the stage management course at our drama school. Jo… no, that name didn't ring any bells. Presumably a girl with that spelling unless Faith had forgotten to put an 'e' at the end. Oh, wait I remember her now. Jo with no 'e' and a ring through her nose.

Didn't remember much about her except I thought we got along just fine when we worked on the same show.

Chapter Twenty-Six

Playing the Field

We were half way through the morning's rehearsal when I remembered more about Jo from drama school. She'd been petite at drama school and sort of punkie with long dyed pink hair or was it blue? Or both. Kind of punkie. Kind of sarf' London. Now she was even smaller than petite. Not anorexic thin but not even petite any more.

It was when we'd just broken midway through the morning to make a cup of tea which in some large scale theatres might have been the job of an assistant stage manager but we didn't have one of those and being a democratic sort of bloke I was making the tea for everyone.

"Two sugars, please, big boy." said Jo and I tensed, slightly startled as she gave my waist a squeeze from behind.

"You don't remember me, do you. From drama school," she said and there was a hint of a challenge in the way she said it.

"Sure I do. I don't remember what show we did together but I remember giving you a ride home one night on the back of my motorcycle."

"Chekhov's *Three Sisters*. I was stage manager. You was Baron Tuzenbach and you was in love with Faith."

"Sorry?"

"You was in love with the character Faith was playing but she wasn't in love with you. What was her name, Faith? Your character in the thing about three sisters?"

"Irina."

"That's the one," Jo said. "I remember there was this luvly moment you had in rehearsal, Ben."

"Me? In Chekhov? Are you sure?"

"Yeah, it was right at the end of the scene. Just before you goes off to fight some stupid duel and you're killed."

"I can imagine that being a good moment. I couldn't stand doing Chekhov so it came as quite a relief to get killed off somewhere in the middle of the play."

"No, but it was luvly, I can still remember it." Clearly nothing was going to stop Jo from telling this story in spite of my efforts to stop her.

Because I did remember. We'd been in two shows together, me and Faith. Not one.

"Anyway", Jo continued. "You and Irina has just sort of said goodbye and you're going off to fight this duel and I don't think she knew that. And you're both walking off the stage going to different places and you just stopped and turned back as if your character wanted to say sumfing else to Irina. Like 'I luv you or sumfing only you didn' have no lines or nuffing so you just turned around and went off to fight the duel and then you were dead after that so you never got the chance to tell her you loved her."

"Sounds like there wasn't a dry seat in the house" Stuart said.

"Don't you mean there wasn't a dry eye in the house?" asked Faith.

"He's being funny. You'll get used to him." I said. "It's part of his charm. Allegedly."

"Anyway it was dead good, what you did. I felt a bit weepy myself. Do you remember that Faith?"

"I don't remember Ben stopping and turning around. The scene was over for me and I think it was our first run through. I was probably desperately trying to remember what my next scene was. Do you remember doing what Jo's talking about?"

"No, not really." But I did remember.

For once as an actor I'd acted purely on instinct. In previous rehearsals I'd pretty much just walked offstage. Maybe hesitantly because I know I'm about to fight a duel and that it's a duel I'm not likely to win. But Jo was bang on the money. Baron Tuzenbach had suddenly been about to say "I love you" for the first time to his wife to be whom he suspects does not feel the same for him. And yet when I turned back towards her to say it, she'd already gone. In fact I could see Faith talking to one of the other actors offstage in the wings.

And so I stood there for a moment looking across the empty stage and I remember feeling very, very alone. And somewhat resigned to Tuzenbach's near certain fate which bizarrely felt very much easier to face for the poor old Baron than running after his fiancée and telling her how he felt. But of course Chekhov didn't write that scene. So Baron Tuzenbach turned around and left the stage never to return.

I remembered that Jake, a Canadian actor who was playing Tuzenbach in the first half of the play was standing in the wings watching me playing his character about to die. He was a bit method was our Jake. And he stopped me in the wings and whispered "That was awesome, man."

Tuzenbach has to play the piano in the first half of the play and Jake had volunteered that he could play a bit. He was a can-do kind of guy, Jake. The kind of guy who might think 'Play the piano? How hard can that be?'

We'd all just found out earlier in that run through how hard that could be because Jake couldn't play a note. And you thought Chekhov couldn't be funny.

"Yeah, that was bloody awesome what you did in rehearsals that day. Even when you didn't have no lines or nuffing."

"Well, if you can't improve on silence" I said. "Every dog has his day."

"Anyway it was dead good." said Jo.

"And for anyone watching it was good you were dead almost immediately afterwards," said Stuart. "Enough of the Benjamin Braddock appreciation society. It's really not a spectator sport. Let's get back to work."

And, yes, I did remember giving Jo a ride home one night after rehearsals. Maybe it was that same night when she'd been so moved by my performance. I could vividly remember when Jo was on the back of my motorbike with her hands around my waist she practically dry humped me on the way home. That was quite a moving performance too.

Act Two of this performance began when I gave her a ride home in my little red sports car after we went to the pub at the end of rehearsals. Only we didn't just dry hump this time.

Chapter Twenty-Seven

Playing Around

Unaccustomed as I was to waking up next to a warm body in the morning I felt a couple of parts of my anatomy reaching for the sky… like the corners of my mouth. Let's keep it clean, people!

But talk about fifty shades of grin…

The corners of my mouth seemed fixed in an upwards trajectory. Without a mirror I could only assume it was an expression of smug, self satisfaction. Not something I practised on a daily basis but it felt pretty damn good, yes, sir, you betcha. There's life in the old dog yet.

Also raised upward was my right eyebrow as I mentally ran through a list of Roger Moore's oh-so-double-oh-seven *double entendres* that seemed appropriate for the occasion. Especially given the ease and speedy progress of this recent coupling.

"What do you think you're doing, Bond?"

"Just keeping the British end up, sir."

Watching old Bond films of the Connery and Moore eras it's difficult to fathom the sheer corniness of their chat up lines. It's also difficult to account for how easy it seems for Bond to shag some girl he's only just met. Almost as implausible as some dishy bird falling for the unlikely charms of Austin Powers. "Yeah, baby!" Almost as hard to fathom as… well, how the hell I'd ended up in bed with Jo. I hadn't suddenly become irresistible to women and I wasn't aware of any recent upsurge in my mojo.

If I was going to analyse the mating habits of the lesser spotted Benjamin Braddock I'd have to conclude that the harder he tried the less likely it was to happen. So how the hell had this come about? Near as I could remember it was something like this.

Act Two, Scene One: Flirtation in the rehearsal room that was more obvious looking back retrospectively than at the time.

Act Two, Scene Two: The scene opens in the cosy back room of the Prince of Wales pub. Director and stage manager are sat close together. Close enough for the occasional brushing of knees. More flirtatious chat turbo-charged by a small but sufficient sufficiency of alcohol. You know the old saying. Candy's dandy but liquor's quicker.

Act Two, Scene Three: Driving Jo home. Is something about to happen here, wonders the audience? The driver of the car is wondering the same thing. Back at Jo's she gets out the car and asks me if I missed having a motor bike and before I could say "not very much" she throws her arms around my neck and her legs around my waist and announces that we have some unfinished business. Business she was very much keen on finishing and she wanted to start finishing it right away.

In the interests of decency we shall skip what acts took place in Act Three, Scenes One through Four and move on to the following morning.

All things considered, it had been quite an unusual year thus far, I thought.

Jo reached for my arm and pulled me closer to her. Spooning when you haven't done it for a while is a blissful way to start the day though in Jo's case it was more like spooning a teaspoon. And then I remembered something else I'd forgotten about Jo. She sometimes sucked her thumb. Truly a woman in a child's frame though she'd proved herself to be more than enough woman for me last night. Her hips had been a blur. More than once, though you could barely count the first time.

Don't judge. This hadn't happened to me in a very long time and I'm not the man I used to be. Truth be told, I probably never was.

Yes, the more heavily in love with someone I was, the more gauche and awkward I was likely to be. Completely silent and unable, when you got down to it, to tell any girl I cared about how I felt. Which of course made it ever so unlikely that me and the said (or unsaid) girl would ever get down to it.

Why couldn't I be more like that guy I used to know who could walk up to a girl he'd never met at a party and say "You look gorgeous. Are you busy for the next twenty minutes because I thought we could get down to some sweet, sweet loving. You know… sex." And he wasn't much of a looker, our Duncan. Drunken Duncan, we called him. More attention to dental hygiene than Austin Powers but definitely more Harry Palmer than Bond, James Bond.

Come to think of it, Drunken Duncan always carried breath freshener spray, because he was a smoker like Michael Caine, whom I read is never without a breath freshener spray in case he has to kiss a girl on a movie set. And if the girl asked what it was he'd say "Here, try some." And Duncan used to do the same trick. Maybe it had some sort of Pavlovian power along the lines of 'We've both got nice, fresh breath now, so let's shag. Yeah, baby!'

Why couldn't I be more like Duncan and less like Mr Darcy, seemingly aloof and immune to the charms of Miss Bennet with one 't'. I always wondered if that's why he was so reluctant to marry outside his class, to marry beneath him. When it came down to it the Bennet family couldn't spell Bennett.

Perhaps if the 't' in Bennet had been silent. If they had pronounced it like it was French. Then we could skip most of that chick lit novel and any number of awful film adaptations and get to the bit where D'Arcy reveals what's been making the bulge in his britches for the last two and a half hours.

What made this story of a frankly annoying little girl falling for some posh bloke who couldn't be more cold and aloof if he were batting for the other side so popular? Come to think of it who knows? If Mr and Mrs Bennet had not sired just daughters and Miss Elizabeth's sister, Jane, had been a fine strapping lad called John the whole saga could have been completely different.

Actually that sounded like quite a good idea for a spoof. A parody that might have legs. It would certainly light a fire under the Jane Austen Book Club. If I could just move my arm, I thought, I could reach for the pencil and note pad beside the bed. Something that would come as a relief as I was fast losing any feeling in the arm and leg underneath Jo's small form. Small but decidedly firm. Absolutely no cushion for the pushin' as *Spinal Tap* would say.

What if I'd told Faith in French what I felt. Would she now be in my bed next to me instead of Jo? Probably not. Faith spoke fluent Southall but French? Not likely. European languages were probably not a big thing for her.

I think that trick only worked on women you'd just met. And were French.

But why the hell couldn't I be more Austin Powers, less Austin Allegro? Why couldn't I be more like Jo in fact? If you saw someone you fancied you just said, "How about it? You fancy a spot of uncomplicated sex for a bit or what?"

And why was my mind wandering from one subject to another when there was a warm body next to me? Don't question it, just go with the flow for once in your life. Enjoy the here and now.

Maybe it would be fun to spend time with someone who was so uncomplicated. To be in a relationship that was so uncomplicated. It had certainly been fun so far. She wasn't the love of my life. She wasn't Faith. But the whole Faith thing hadn't been any fun at all.

Maybe it would be safer to be involved with Jo for a while. A sort of anti-Faith medication. Safer and a lot

148

of fun which was about to resume as Jo turned round and kissed me.

'Space shuttle to mission control… permission to launch? Good God, what's Bond up to now? I think he's attempting re-entry, sir,' I thought.

"Oh behave, Mrs Kensington!" I said.

"Who's Mrs Kensington?"

"It's an Austin Powers gag. Not important."

"I like him. He's funny. Hey, why don't you put your glasses on?"

"I thought girls don't make passes at men who wear glasses."

"Well, this girl's about to have sex with a man wearing specs."

"Yeah, baby! Let's shag!"

"Oh Austin…"

"Oh Mrs Kensington… Quick question. Do you like Jane Austen?"

"Can't stand her."

"Cool."

"We had to read that shit at school. So boring… How's my breath by the way?"

"It's just fine, Jo. It's just fine."

Chapter Twenty-Eight

Play Back

Judy	I'm going to be late back tonight. Can you pick up the twins?
Stuart	Can't your mother do it?
Judy	Again?
Stuart	Like she's got anything better to do.
Judy	Why can't you do it?
Stuart	Doing something with Dai.
Judy	What?
Stuart	I said I'm doing something with Dai.
Judy	I heard. I meant what are you doing with Dai?

Stuart	Usual stuff. He wanted to talk about where to take the show next.
	Judy says nothing.
Stuart	Something about doing it live. Live on stage. Like the old days. Like we used to do way back when.
	Judy says nothing.
Stuart	What?
Judy	I didn't say anything.
Stuart	I know. Your silence is deafening.
Judy	You're going to see that little tart, aren't you. The one from make-up.
Stuart	Who from make-up? Not Monica, she's gay for God's sake.

Judy	No, not Monica. Obviously. The other one. The one you've been screwing for… I don't know. You tell me. How long have you been screwing her, Stuart? How long?

Pause.

Stuart	Who told you?

Judy says nothing.

Stuart	Who fucking told you? It was Dai, wasn't it? I'm going to get that little bastard for this?

Judy	It wasn't Dai. It wasn't anybody… I didn't know until now. God, your a bastard aren't you.

Stuart	Yes, your mother was right all along.

Judy slaps Stuart.

"Sorry can we stop a second." said Faith.
"Sure, what's up? I asked.

"I think it's great that we're getting it on it's feet so soon. I'm just not comfortable slapping Stuart."

"Just at this point in the play or in general?" I asked.

"I'd just like to practise it so I don't hurt him."

"Just do it for real" Stuart said. "I like a bit of rough."

"Oh shush, Stuart" said Faith. "You are awful."

"But you like me," said Stuart.

"Enough of the seventies comedy catchphrases, Stuart. So how do you want to do this, Faith?"

"Slowly."

"And often," I said. "Let's see you two rehearse the slap until I get tired of seeing Stuart get slapped."

"We could practise it alone if you like" said Stuart said, sidling up to Faith. "Just you and me, see."

"Worst Humphrey Bogart impression ever." I said.

"I never saw a dame yet that didn't understand a good slap in the mouth or a slug from a '45."

"My mistake, second worst Humphrey Bogart impression ever."

"God, listen to the two of you. You're just like the two guys in the play," said Faith.

"I'm glad you said that." I said." That's exactly what I was going for."

"So did real Stuart always, always get the girl in real life?" asked Faith.

"Yup," said real Stuart.

"If I ever looked like I was about to get lucky with a girl, he had a photo of me aged twelve that he carried in his wallet."

"God, you really are awful, Stuart," said Faith.

"But in a good way," said Stuart."I was doing the the girls a favour."

"He used to ask the girl if she wanted to know what our kids would look like. And then he'd show them the photo."

"And you carried it about with you?"

"Never left home without it," said Stuart.

"And you've got it on you right now?" asked Jo, looking up from making notes in the rehearsal diary.

"Of course," said Stuart. "You never know when you're going to need it."

Stuart started reaching into his wallet for the umpteenth time and produced the photo of me aged twelve, which had so often seen more action than I ever did. It was almost not one photo but two, torn in the middle.

"God, it's a bit faded, innit?" said Jo.

"Well, so's he," said Stuart. "I mean, look at him."

"I think Ben looks gorgeous now," said Jo. "Don't he look gorgeous, Faith?"

"Yeah, I can absolutely believe that Judy would go for him now."

"Well, maybe on stage, "said Stuart. "Lots of make-up… If he was lit from behind. It's what do you call it?… Suspension of disbelief, isn't it."

"Say it isn't so, Jo," said Faith.

Pause…

"While we're stopped anyway I'd rather not say the word 'fucking' in this scene," said Stuart.

"Not grammatically correct enough for you." I asked.

"I'd just rather not say it."

"I'm asking you to say it, not do it."

"Doing it would be fine. I just don't want to say it."

"You're a strangely moral person for a sleazebag," I said.

"Well, while you're coming up with some synonyms for the word "fucking" I'm going to have a pee." And off he went.

"There are no synonyms for fucking," I shouted after him. "That's the point. Sometimes it's just the right word you're looking for."

"I agree with you," said Jo. "Keep the 'fucking' in. Hundred per cent. I'm going for a pee too. Back in a mo." And out she went.

"Speaking of fucking," said Faith as the door closed behind Jo. "I'm very happy for you."

"Excuse me?"

"You and you know who." And she gave my arm a little squeeze.

"Does everybody know?"

"Not yet. But they will. It's so 'fucking' obvious."

Chapter Twenty-Nine

A Play within a Play

"So, Player," said Fiona, pouring me a glass of chardonnay.

"Just a small one."

"Not what I heard. Mr Player… The play's the thing wherein I'll catch the thingy of the King."

"You've lost me," I said. "I don't follow."

"A play within a play?… Clever. Nice play, Player. *Well played.*"

"Enough. Playtime's over. Who told you?"

"Stuart."

"Oh God everybody really does know then. Or will do shortly."

"So when do I get to meet her. Jo, is it?"

"Jo, yes."

"Why didn't you bring her tonight? Is she some sort of ghastly little troll? A shameful secret? Did she put the troll in trollop?"

"She does perhaps have some engaging troll-like qualities. She's very small for one thing. And she doesn't believe in shaving her arm pits."

"The little troll… How about?… You know… South of the border?"

"Currently doesn't shave there either but say's she's gone both ways in the past."

"The little trollop…"

"In fact she said it was up to me."

"And did the gentleman express any preference?"

"Being a gentleman I really can't tell you."

"Oh come on, Ben you must have an opinion on the subject."

"I said I was more of a traditionalist."

"So matching collar and cuffs."

"Exactly."

"You little devil, you."

"Although to be completely accurate in terms of trim downstairs she's short back and sides with a colour scheme of red, white, and blue."

"A patriot then."

"She said that once she'd trimmed and shaved it in the shape of a little love heart."

"She sounds sweet. I like her."

"I think she'd like you too. She said in the past she's gone both ways in that regard too."

"And how do you feel about that?"

"A threesome? I'd be too embarrassed."

"I should keep Stuart on a need to know basis in that regard. He'd be all up for it."

"Jo wondered if she went with a girl if that was cheating."

"Without you present you mean?"

"Precisely."

"And what did you wonder about that?"

"I wondered that would most definitely be cheating."

"Good for you. So maybe not a keeper but a keeper for right now."

"That's what I'm thinking. Feeling a bit guilty about that though, to tell you the truth."

"Do tell."

"I'm not sure how I feel about Faith now."

"I know I'm going to regret this but… do tell. Just the up to date stuff. You've thoroughly bored me about all the drama school dramatics and I only have the one bottle of chardonnay in the fridge."

"Cutting down?

"Yes. You?"

"Me too. Spending time with Jo helps out of an evening. One bottle of Bacardi Breezer and she's out for the count."

"One bottle… You mentioned she was small, I think."

"Very."

"What are we talking here? Pocket size?"

"Jo? Very nearly."

"Bacardi Breezer, you say?"

"That's all she drinks."

"Oh dear. Is she terribly common?"

"Purley . She's from Purley."

"And she's a goer. Say no more."

"Nudge, nudge ,wink, say no more… No, seriously. Say no more. Seriously. Please. This interrogation's getting a bit personal and a little tiresome."

"She's beginning to sound like Eliza Doolittle. Are you planning to play Professor Higgins to her flower girl?"

"She can't sing."

"Neither could Audrey Hepburn."

"Jo's no Audrey Hepburn. One of those was quite tall, the other is quite small."

"And Faith?"

"Sings like Julie Andrews, talks more like Southall but not so much since she went to drama school. Sounds posh for Southall now if there is such a thing."

"But didn't attend finishing school is what you're saying."

"Not in Switzerland, no. Not like you dear."

"Alright, tell me more about Faith and then tell me more about Jo. Should I put another bottle of wine in the fridge?"

"Not on my account."

"Noticed any difference in your general demeanour since cutting back on the sauce?"

"I've had a lot more sex… But I'm not sure which way round it goes. The connection between sex and sobriety. It's the classic chicken and egg paradox."

"Increased sobriety might have a positive effect on the quality as well as the frequency."

"Perhaps, yes."

"It's definitely put you in a better mood."

"Which? Sex or increased sobriety?"

"Both. Though I was talking about the reduction in your slightly out of hand drinking thing. You've always liked a little drinky-poo and you have occasionally had sex since I've known you, but I'd say it's the drink reduction that's at the bottom of it. You're not so broody, so inward looking. And if being with Jo means less of the one and more of the other I'd say all things considered this Jo thing is a good idea. If not forever, at least for now."

"And they said romance was dead. And speaking of romance how are things with the racing driver?"

"Initially racy but then he went back to being James Hunt. A complete hunt in fact. So I dumped him."

"Sorry to hear that. So this is a bit of a turn up for the books. I'm getting some and no one else is."

"Stuart?"

"Things have been pretty quiet on the barmaid circuit. He isn't even talking about it."

"It?"

"IT. Getting it."

"Ah…. IT… That's not like Stuart."

"Not at all."

"Is he ill?"

"Don't think so. He comes to rehearsals. Knows his lines surprisingly well. He's almost off book. Which is early for him. Mostly just goes straight home at the end of the night though we went out a couple of times last week, the four of us. Come to think of it, I didn't get any stick from Stuart about me and Jo, which is not like him."

"Maybe he's happy for you."

"Come on, this is Stuart we're talking about."

"He's not quite as bad you made him out to be in the play."

"He's not actually capable of murder as far as I know. I'll grant you that. Did I tell you I had that dream again?"

"The one where you think you're being followed by the mysterious hooded figure?"

"That's the one?"

"Shown his face yet?"

"Not so far. I'm just hoping it's not Death."

"Death?"

"The Grim Reaper?"

"Any signs of a scythe?"

"Not that I remember."

"Any gardening implements of any kind?"

"None. Thanks for being so sympathetic."

"Feeling menaced by a faceless figure is pretty common, you know. I sometimes have a dream where some huge bloke is on top of me in a dark room with loads of candles and he's doing some pretty horrible things to me. Let's just say it's less than consensual. But I can never see his face. I can smell his bad breath but I can never see his face."

"Think you've been watching too much *Game of Thrones.*"

"No, there's never any dragons."

"Think it was James Hunt? The guy in the dream?"

"No, he was into some pretty kinky stuff but, to be fair to him, his oral hygiene was immaculate."

"He did have nice teeth."

"See? Everyone else's fears and nightmares are just a bit of fun to everyone else."

"That's all very well but you're not living under a sentence of death."

"The psychic thing again? I thought you were over that."

"A death sentence does keep you up at nights if you're the one under it."

"I thought it was mainly Jo who kept you up at nights?"

"Funny. Very funny. Seriously it's not much fun sitting under the sword of Damocles."

"Sword of what now?"

"The sword of Damocles. It's an old legend. Damocles thinks the King is a really lucky guy because he's got all this power and wealth. So the King arranges for Damocles to sit on the throne for a day but he suspends a bloody great sword over Damocles' head and it's suspended by a single hair from a horse's tail.?"

"And the moral of the story is?"

" I don't know. With great wealth and power comes great danger and great responsibility?"

"Or if you see a sword hanging over a chair, don't sit on the chair."

"It's like the psychic guy said. Great wealth and great danger. His two predictions."

"Of which only one has come true so far."

"So far."

"He probably just got lucky with the first one. What makes you think you're in any danger?"

"My sister called again."

"Kate?"

"Yes"

"What's she calling herself these days."

"Back to Kate."

"Not Katie?"

"No, she was briefly Kaye but never Katie. Not so far."

"And is she dangerous?"

"No, mad but not dangerous. But apparently my brother thinks I owe him money for something or other. And he is dangerous."

"And do you?"

"Owe him anything? Not as far as I recall. I think he's just jealous that suddenly I've got money. I was always the poor relation and he always had pots of money. I think that made him feel better about himself."

"He's the pilot, yes?"

"Was. He's on a sick pension now but he's basically a drunk. That's how he got sick."

"Said the pot calling the kettle black."

"Who's still on his first glass of chardonnay, please note."

"Do you know there's something else I've noticed tonight. Maybe it's your relative sobriety but you're sharper. You're clearer. You don't drone on quite so much."

"Drone on?"

"Yes, not to put too fine a point on it but when you're drinking too much you do go on a bit. Let's just say some of your sentences used to start to sound like an acceptance speech at the Oscars. There's still a lot of references to films and television but maybe slightly less now that you're starting to live life a little more. You're less on the sidelines looking on. You're in the game."

"The game of life. The sad thing is when I'm part way through telling a story, even part way through a sentence, I can tell the other person's losing interest."

"Losing the will to live sometimes."

"You should hear my brother. He once ranted on the phone to me for three hours. During the last hour I did not make a sound. Not one. No acknowledgement that there was someone listening to him at the end of the line. At one point I got up and made myself a sandwich and when I came back to the phone he was still talking. He was completely unaware that I'd been away from the phone."

"Doesn't make him dangerous. Sounds like he might just be lonely."

"Lonely? More like psychotic. You can be both, I guess. He used to send me thousands of abusive texts. I had to block him. Haven't spoken to him in years."

"And so now he's jealous that you're a millionaire?"

"According to Kate. No, she didn't say he was jealous. She just said he's raging about something to do with me. I said 'What's new?' Let's talk about something else other than my family before I really do need another glass of wine."

"You haven't caught me up on how Faith is. She's married now, right?"

"I don't know if they're actually married or it's just a partnership or whatever but she's got a couple of kids. Both just started school or nursery, I think. They're like four and seven."

"Domestic bliss then."

"I guess. She doesn't say much. Sometimes has to go home early to pick up the kids but rehearsals are going so well that it scarcely matters. Stuart and she are really nailing it. First time with almost every scene. I hardly have to do or say a thing as director. It's like they're not playing it, they're living it."

"Sounds like she's bringing the best out of Stuart."

"As an actor, sure. I guess that's the thing about good actors. They make other people look good too."

"You find the same thing in dance."

"That's what it's like. That's exactly what it's like. It's like watching the two of them dance."

"I can't wait to see it."

"I just hope I can keep up with the two of them."

"It'll be fine, Ben. I'm sure you'll all be great together. And by the way. Better trousers. Not saggy at all."

Chapter Thirty

Play the Ball

"I have to say, Ben, you were absolutely right about Faith," said Stuart. "Fore!"

Stuart's golf ball bounced twice before perfectly bisecting the ten feet gap separating the elderly couple on the green of the first par three.

"I did say you should have waited longer."

The man was holding the flag for his wife as Stuart's ball picked up speed on the downslope and went though the green. The woman missed her putt and immediately turned towards Stuart and myself on the third tee. Stuart was still holding the pose at the end of his follow through.

"I'm hitting them pretty sweetly today, don't you think?"

"You nearly hit them sweetly."

"Bloody hooligans," shouted the elderly gentleman. "I shall report you."

"We're not members," Stuart shouted back.

"And you never will be," thundered the old man.

"He's got a good set of lungs, hasn't he? For an old geezer," said Stuart.

Stuart and I don't play golf very often though we both learned to play as kids. Our fathers were keen amateur golfers who regularly competed against each other in amateur medals. That's a competition run by golf clubs for amateur players if you're not a follower of the game and prefer your good walks unspoilt. In our games we generally play holes rather than count strokes as is the norm in the professional game. This means if your opponent is two up with three to play that means he has won two more holes than you after fifteen holes, so there are only three holes left and you're in all likelihood about to lose unless you're Tiger Woods and can storm home by winning the last three holes.

Golf in the main is still regarded as something of a gentlemen's game. I would add "with apologies to the ladies" to that sentence but golf is often also spectacularly misogynistic and racist. If you're either black, Jewish or female there are golf clubs galore where you were not welcome even in the recent past and probably that's true even today.

To combat this gentlemen's club stuffiness Stuart delights in flouting almost all of golf's conventions like waiting till the group of players ahead have cleared the green on a short par three before you tee off. His frequent cry of "fore", a foreshortening of the word "before" is meant to be a polite warning (apology implied) if your golf ball ever threatens the well-being of the group ahead. With Stuart it's more of a roar of triumph. I sometimes wonder if he confuses golf with ten pin bowling. It's thoroughly irresponsible and downright dangerous but Stuart has proved himself completely impervious to my attempts in the past to rein in his behaviour. According to my dad, Stuart's father was just the same and I guess the acorn doesn't fall far from the tree.

And it's not just the way he plays but also the way he dresses. Wildly flamboyant would not begin to cover it. Today's ensemble consisted of a tangerine silk shirt (untucked) and a pair of lime green trousers with a repeating motif of large yellow bananas. I have no idea where he buys these outfits. Perhaps there's some dark corner of the internet where he finds them.

"So how are things with Jo, dare I ask?"

"I'm surprised you didn't ask before."

"Well, how's it going?"

"It's going... fine."

Neither Stuart are I are great at golf. The occasional good shot is an oasis of calm in a sea of disappointment as a series of hooks and slices punctuate our game. Good players can manipulate the ball with a draw or a gentle fade so that it gently moves to the left or right in flight in a controlled manner to negotiate hazards like trees or bunkers. With duff golfers like the two of us it's mostly either a snap hook or a wild slice. Quite a different thing altogether. Not so much a gentle deliberate movement in the air as a sharp uncontrolled parabolic curve. Almost equally maddening is the occasional good shot straight down the middle of the fairway which leads you to think 'how the hell did I do that?' and 'why can't I do it more often?'

Stuart tends to hook them left and I tend to slice them right which means our on course conversations are relatively short or punctuated by a series of

168

interruptions while one of us searches for our ball in the woods on the right while the other tries to dig his ball out of the bunker on the left.

On this occasion, however, we'd hit our balls in more or less the same direction with my ball having come to rest six feet short of the green and Stuart's twenty yards further on the same line on the downslope on the far side of the green, just short of some perilously thick rough. Even Stuart's worst shots seem to land in a spot where he can still play the ball rather than in a gorse bush or a stream. I have never seen him lose a ball. I on the other hand have been known to lose six balls in a single round.

"So and Jo… Just fine?"

"Yeah. Just Fine."

"Not going to tell me any more?"

"No."

By this time I'd reached my ball. In golf etiquette it is the height of rudeness to speak when your opponent is getting ready to hit the ball and even Stuart observes this rule. He does go perilously close to transgressing though and likes to indulge in what one recent Australian cricket captain called 'mental disintegration' of your opponent. Stuart's apparently casual next remark as I got a pitching wedge out my bag was therefore not a friendly piece of advice but carefully calculated to make me fluff my next shot.

"Watch out for the downslope. You don't want to end up where I am."

Fully determined not to end up where he was by hitting a confident chip that might roll past the hole and leave me with an uphill putt, which is always easier than a downhill one, I duly fluffed my shot. My ball barely made it on to the putting surface.

"Oh bad luck", said Stuart. "Still at least you're on the green."

"Thanks."

"Are you seeing her tonight?" Stuart asked.

"Maybe. Why did you want to do something?"

"No, I think I'll just have a quiet night in." said Stuart.

"You've been having a lot of those lately."

"I suppose. Just haven't felt like going out."

"Not like you."

"I'll be lucky to get this one close," he said with a little waggle of his hips like a duck shaking water off its bum and a matching waggle with the club head over the ball which preceded his every shot and never ceased to annoy me. Stuart at least looks like a golfer with a club in his hand whereas my swing is less extravagant and somewhat unnatural and manufactured. There's a glorious freedom to Stuart's golf swing which means when he gets it right he hits the ball a mile. My good shots don't go half as far and their only good quality is that they're sometimes relatively straight. Stuart could in fact probably be quite good at golf if he put his mind to it or played more often.

"I think she's a keeper." Stuart came out of his stance and gave me a broad smile.

"Jo? Really?"

"Yes, really." The broad smile came out once more. "You've been much happier since you started slipping her one."

"You had to go and spoil the mood, didn't you." Stuart began to address the ball once more. To most golfers this means you're getting ready to play your shot. Stuart takes this rather more literally on occasion when the pressure's on and actually does address the ball.

"Nice ball… Good ball…"

"Fiona said much the same the same thing, more or less," I said.

"Please don't talk when I'm about to play. It's frightfully bad form, don't you know."

Stuart proceeded to loft the ball and it floated through the air and bounced a few feet short. Irritatingly it came to rest about ten inches from the hole. Stuart might have been somewhat erratic with a driver but his short game was comparatively deadly. 'Drive for show, putt for dough' was his favourite way of undermining my confidence if I ever hit a half decent tee shot.

"I'll give you that one," I said and tossed him the ball. He was never going to miss a putt like that. Stuart still uses his father's old wooden shafted putter which looks like it belongs in a museum but in Stuart's hands still operated with surgical precision.

"Thanks very much, old chap. That's me two up, I think." He didn't think nothing. Stuart always knew what the score was between us and how many shots we'd both taken on any particular hole.

If you've ever seen the black and white film, *School for Scoundrels* (much better than the re-make), and I know Stuart has, you'll be familiar with the concepts of gamesmanship and oneupmanship. The art of getting one up on your opponent in order to win the game or get the girl. You'll also remember the villain of the piece played by the gap-toothed Terry-Thomas. He was the archetypal old school bounder and cad who will do anything to win and retain alpha-male status in any situation. Stuart could have been a visiting professor at the School of Lifemanship. By this point he was doing just about everything apart from cackling and twirling an imaginary moustache. "I know it's my honour but you go ahead. I'm just going to have a pee." Stuart does this every time we play. I'm not sure if it's another ruse to put me off or if he's just marking his territory as the dominant male. There were some convenient bushes next to the tee which Stuart proceeded to fertilise. I got out my shiny new driver. I had treated myself to some top of the line clubs in the hope that they were going to help my game and this was the first time I'd used them in anger. Anger was the operative word since I was starting to get more than usually annoyed by Stuart's antics. His behaviour was expected but seemed to have an added edge today.

"Long par four this next hole. If you can manage a slight pull to the left that will help you round those trees. Assuming you get it that far. Better give it some welly. Grip it and rip it."

"Thanks for the tip, Tiger." I said without any semblance of sincerity.

Any amateur golfer will tell you that if you consciously try to hit the ball hard the resulting shot is seldom a thing of beauty . Predictably I hit another wild slice and my ball went deep into the woods on the right.

"Oh bad luck,"said Stuart.

He was still behind me when I was taking my swing so I couldn't be sure but I'd swear he hadn't even looked up to see where my ball went. He was still giving his trouser snake a shake before tucking it away when I turned around in impotent fury. It was as if he'd simply assumed that somewhere in the trees was the inevitable destination of my ball. I was tempted to wrap the damn club round his neck but physical conflict is never my thing so I bottled up my feelings as usual. The golf ball would continue to be the only victim of my violent intent which was of course entirely Stuart's intention.

"Let's have a shot with those fancy new clubs of yours," said Stuart. "What's that you're got there, a driver? Let me have a go with that."

We both knew this was a classic ploy from the school of oneupmanship. Stuart often offers to swap tennis rackets around the time I am a set and four-love down. I actually look quite good when I play tennis though I don't hit the ball very hard. Stuart looks robotic by comparison and has no backhand to speak of but he counters this by running round his backhand to return my pretty but powder puff shots to hit a series of thunderous forehand winners.

I have never beaten him at tennis. In tennis, as with golf and girls, Stuart is very competitive.

I handed Stuart my new driver with a barely audible sigh of precognition at the seemingly inevitable outcome. Stuart didn't just hit his next shot far and straight. He hit it somewhere near the county of Middlesex. And we were in Surrey. I think it was the best shot I'd ever seen him play. I was speechless.

"Nothing wrong with the clubs," said Stuart. "Maybe you just have to get used to them."

"Actually I'm thinking of giving up golf."

"But that would only leave you with strangling animals and masturbation as hobbies."

"And cricket."

"You haven't played in years."

"I'm seriously thinking of taking it up again."

"Since when?"

"About ten minutes ago."

Two immaculately attired golfers were by now patiently waiting to tee off behind us.

"Why don't you two play through," I said. "My ball's in the woods."

Stuart and I began to walk up the right side of the fairway while the other two golfers hit their shots arrow straight up the favourable left hand side of the fairway. These two were obviously regular players but their drives barely reached Stuart's.

"I hate when you do that. Let other players play through," Stuart said.

This was not news to me.

"Just being polite," I said.

"A minor victory" I thought.

It might surprise you to know that Stuart always helps me look for my ball on such occasions. True, he has an uncanny knack of finding other people's abandoned balls as well and I doubt very much if he has ever had to buy a golf ball. He often finds mine before I do and, if he can't find it, I generally accept that it's lost and play another one from it's estimated position. Stuart and I don't play strict rules of golf but strangely enough he always seems to be more familiar with our informal rules than I am and will confidently announce that I can move the ball one club's length but will lose a shot and also have to buy the first round in the clubhouse.

My ball was proving particularly elusive on this occasion.

"You know you were absolutely right about Faith, Ben?"

"What do you mean?"

"In rehearsal. Playing opposite her. She's amazing. It's like it's real. Like you're doing it for real. She's just so natural."

"I told you, didn't I? Actually I was a bit worried about you."

"About me? Why?" asked Stuart.

"Whether the two of you would hit it off. You're both so different.

"As people you mean?"

"Well, that too come to think of it, but I meant as actors, really."

"Opposites attract. I think that's what I like about your play. Judy has no business being with a stinker like me in the play. The audience is rooting for good old Dai to get the girl. They're rooting for Dai and Judy. But yeah, she's a knockout in rehearsals. You've really got to bring your A-game. Hell, I didn't even mind doing that crazy improv you came up with. The two of us washing the dishes together."

"The idea just came to me when were about to break for tea. I think it was a really useful exercise."

"I thought it was the dumbest idea you'd ever come up with but it really worked. I think it really gave us the feeling that, for all our differences, we had been a partnership. A team. Husband and wife."

"It was like you were dancing," I said.

"You've got the heart and soul of a poet, Ben. I've always said that."

"You've never said that. Somebody else once did but it wasn't you."

"Well, I'm saying it now."

"Well, I'm really excited with how it's going in rehearsals. I didn't want to say it in so many words. I didn't want to jinx it."

By this point I was using a short iron like a scythe to try to find my ball in the undergrowth. Stuart was using his more stealthy and successful approach of using his eyes.

"Found another one," said Stuart.

"Mine?"

176

"Afraid not. You look like the Grim Reaper. That's a pitching wedge in your hand not a whatchamacallit."

"A scythe? Please let's not talk about the Grim Reaper, can we?"

"Sore subject?"

"Yes."

"Still?"

"Yes. Still."

I wiped some sweat off my brow from the exertions of swinging the club.

"I give up. I think I'm going to have to play another ball," I said.

"Actually your ball is just behind you. I found it five minutes ago but I was enjoying our little chat."

"You could have told me that before."

"It wouldn't have been funny before."

I shook my head in disbelief as I settled over the ball with the club I already had in my hand. It seemed as likely an implement as any to get the ball out from where it was since I didn't have anything resembling a shovel in my golf bag.

I took a wild hack at the ball more in hope than with any well thought out plan. The ball flew with surprising speed, ricocheting off two trees, nearly missing Stuart the first time and hitting him a painful blow on the ankle on its return before landing almost exactly where it started.

"Fore!" I shouted.

"Jesus Christ, you could have killed me," said Stuart.

"I think I'm starting to get the hang of these clubs," I said.

Stuart moved into a position behind a tree where he calculated he would be completely safe from my next shot. I made a much cleaner connection this time and the ball flew sweetly off the club face. It seemed to hang for an eternity, heading straight in line with the hole before landing short and plugging deep in a large bunker protecting the front of the green.

"Oh bad luck."

"Stuart, one of these days…" Knowing that this was just the sort of response Stuart wished to provoke, I decided against expressing what I had in mind.

"He's on the beach!" said Stuart.

I recognised the quote but couldn't name the film which annoyed me just that little bit more, if that were possible.

"If you tell me I'd better put on sunscreen and a hat because I'm going to be there for some time, your life will be in danger," I said as we walked over to Stuart's ball, just left of centre on the fairway ahead of us. Stuart hit another immaculate chip shot to the centre of the green.

Memo to self. Must pay for golf lessons from a professional. I'm going to beat Stuart at this bloody game if it's the last thing I do.

"Fancy a game of tennis at the weekend?" asked Stuart.

"No."

Chapter Thirty-One

Play Date

Famously the third date is supposed to be the one you get lucky on if you're going to get lucky at all. This left me with a bit of a conundrum with Jo because we'd already done the dirty but hadn't actually been on a date yet, assuming your definition of a date is boy meets girl, boy takes girl to dinner and a movie, boy kisses girl good night and goes home horny.

I'm pretty sure going for drinks after work with your colleagues doesn't count as a date and that's essentially the closest Jo and I had been to going on one. Without going through any dating formalities we'd already coupled up several times in the bedroom and other places. But let's not go all Cluedo here and go into who did what to whom using a length of rope in the conservatory. Don't be mucky. For one thing, I don't have a conservatory.

It always surprised me that there was no bathroom in the house featured in the board game, Cluedo. As far as I know nobody has ever been killed in a billiard room although if you've played snooker with Stuart this may come as a surprise. To my certain knowledge a number of people have died not just in the bathroom but sitting on or falling off the the toilet. Elvis and Judy Garland, King George II of England and King Wenceslaus III of Bohemia. So that's three kings and a drama queen if you count Elvis and Judy G. And Wenceslaus was actually murdered. By an assassin's spear to be exact, which must surely be a more popular choice of weapon than a candlestick or a length of lead pipe. The identity of Wenceslaus' assassin is unknown but my money is on Professor Plum.

Back in my bathroom Jo and I were taking a shower together and I mustered up sufficient courage to pop the big question. "It's Sunday so do you fancy spending the day together?" Jo did me the honour of accepting my proposal so now we just had to find something we wanted to do together. Apart from the other thing that we'd just done together in the shower. So my question to self was this. If we've already skipped ahead to post-third-date-coitus what the hell were we supposed to do now for our first two dates? We couldn't agree on a movie even though we went through every cinema listing in the Greater London Area. And it was the middle of the day so a romantic candle lit dinner wasn't really an option.

"Let's just go for a drive in your sexy little car."

"We could have a picnic." I said.

"If you like. Can I drive?"

"I thought you didn't have a license."

"I don't."

"Then no. You can't drive."

"Spoil sport."

We couldn't agree on what to buy for the picnic. Jo's idea of a three course meal was apparently two different chocolate bars and a bag of potato chips. We agreed to differ on whether the chips was a vegetable and therefore constituted one of your 5-a-day and I bought myself some smoked salmon, camembert and a baguette. I had to promise Jo that the cheese wouldn't smell like old socks though secretly I hoped it would as that's how I like my camembert. Two non-alcoholic beers and the inevitable Bacardi Breezer completed the Sunday fun day feast.

We did our best to beat the Sunday morning traffic out to the west of London on the M4 motorway. It was slow going until we were past the M25 but then the sun came out and the traffic thinned.

"So what's in this Bray place?"

"Well, Stuart's playing cricket there today for one thing?"

"Cricket? Yawn! Can't stand cricket. Bloody boring game."

"Oh dear. I was thinking of taking it up again."

"You any good?"

"Slightly less good than Stuart."

"Who's he play for?"

"Stage Cricket Club, London theatres. Teams made up of actors."

"Anybody famous?"

"Sean Connery played for London Theatres once, I think."

"When Daniel Craig's playing, you let me know."

"I take it you're not keen."

"Bunch of theatre luvvies playing cricket? Leave it out."

"Okay, we can just have a picnic by the river."

"That sounds more like it. Still boring but better than watching cricket."

"It's a really pretty village."

"So pretty boring then."

"I guess."

"I could show you Monkey Island."

"Where's that then?"

"Middle of the river. Just where you'd expect an island to be."

"Are there monkeys?"

"Not as such, no."

"So why'd they call it Monkey Island."

"Something to do with monks, I think."

"You really know how to show a girl a good time, don't you."

Eventually we found a quiet spot to have our picnic and we settled into our date. It wasn't exactly Brideshead Revisited since I hadn't brought a teddy bear and Jo was wearing a pair of denim cut offs that she liked to refer to as "shag-me-shorts". The camembert was disappointing but the beer was still sort of cold and the Bacardi Breezer reported to be agreeably breezy.

I was just dozing off in the sun with Jo snuggled into my shoulder. I dared to think the date was slowly improving. What I wasn't expecting was the Spanish Inquisition.

"You really fancied Faith at drama school, didn't you."

"Sorry?"

I desperately tried to think of some way of stalling this conversation while I considered what might be an acceptable response to this unexpected question.

"Sort of." Probably not an acceptable response I feared but the best I could come up with.

"How can you sort of fancy someone? Either you do or you don't."

"Sometimes things aren't that simple. Come to think of it I don't think they're ever that simple where I'm concerned."

"So you saying you didn't fancy her?"

"I don't know how to explain it. How do you feel when you see Daniel Craig in a movie."

"Phwoar, wanna get me some of that. That's what I'm thinking. He's bloody gorgeous."

"Not quite the level of subtlety I was hoping for but that's close enough. I had this, I don't know, crush on her, but I think it was her as an actress, not as a person. Does that make sense?"

"No."

"Have you ever seen the film, *Casablanca?* "

"Not you and your bloody films I've never heard of."

"It's like when I see that film, I'm sort of in love with Ilse Lund, or rather the actress playing her, Ingrid Bergman."

I was quite pleased with this analogy as now that I thought about it Faith did look a little like Ingrid Bergman. But now was certainly not the time to linger on that thought.

"Is this film in black and white?"

"Yes."

"Thought so."*

"I'm just trying to explain. Look, maybe I was in love with my idea of Faith but that idea wasn't her. It didn't really exist except I'm my imagination. Nothing could ever have happened between us because I was in love with a phantom. Okay, how's this? It wasn't hard to imagine that Baron Tuzenbach was in love with Irina."

"In love?"

"I chose my words poorly."

"You said it twice."

"Poorly chosen both times. Sorry. Infatuated might be closer to the truth. Look, you've got nothing to worry about on that score."

"I should bloody well hope not."

"In reality Faith and I would have been a disaster. We've got nothing in common."

"And what about us? What've we got in common?"

"We seemed to have found one common interest."

"Yeah, that's true. Think that's enough?"

"It's enough for now."

"It's a start, innit."

"Sure."

"And what about Faith?"

"We'll always have Paris…"

"What?"

"Stupid joke. Forget it."

"You don't half talk some shit sometimes, Ben."

"Sorry about that. Bad habit."

"Just so long as you're not thinking about her when we're at it."

"Couldn't be further from my mind."

"Good."

"Happy?"

"Yeah." She burst out laughing.

"What?"

"It wasn't half funny watching you squirm."

I let Jo sleep for a while before waking her up so we could beat the worst of the traffic heading back into London. We'd just passed Slough, which frankly is the best thing to do if you're passing Slough, when Jo spoke above the slightly throaty roar that told me the the Alfa might need a new exhaust soon. Not a big surprise since the car had spent more time on a mechanic's hoist than it had on the road. Not only did the roof leak when it rained but most of the electrics started to play up whenever there was a hint of moisture in the air. But hey, it was still cute and it was Italian.

"I was having a lovely dream back there by the river."

"What about?"

"You and me. We were in this car."

"This car?"

"This car. This exact car and... have you ever wondered where the expression petrol head came from."

"Why would I... Hey, stop that. We're on the M4. You can't do that."

"Well pull over and I'll show you why they call it the hard shoulder."

In the interests of road safety I pulled over and cut the engine. I discovered that Jo really was something of a petrol head and I began to learn why they called it an Alfa Romeo.

"This car has a unibody construction…" I said

"Tell me more," said Jo

"And a twin cam in-line four cylinder engine…"

"I love it when you talk dirty."

"One of the first cars designed with front and rear… careful with where you're putting your… crumple zones."

"Shut up and do me, Ben."

"Hark, fair Juliet speaks…"

Chapter Thirty-Two

Playing Scared...

Or just scared.

I woke up suddenly with an involuntary sound in my throat like a barking seal and a body spasm that finished in my legs kicking at the bed covers to break free from their embrace.

Barking seal morphed into panting dog. A feverish cold sweat enveloped my head while the rest of my body felt on fire.

Some kind of night terror, I thought as my breathing began to slow even though my heart was still pounding and I had no idea who or what I was trying to kick free from. It's alright, you're awake now, I told myself.

Awake, yes, but where the hell was I?

It looked like your standard hotel room in the ambient streetlight coming through the gap in the curtains which had obviously been cut for economy rather than efficiency. Beyond the unoccupied second queen size bed there was light coming from the door of what I assumed was the bathroom.

I heard the taps turning and then the shower running. "Jo?"

What time is it, I wondered?

I looked over at a radio alarm clock but the numbers were flashing so there had either been a power cut or else I hadn't set it.

That's not like me, I thought. I always joke that I'm right twice a day like a broken clock, but I can't stand seeing a clock that's not set to the right time. If I had a pound for every time I've re-set the clock on other people's microwaves...

I kicked at the remaining knot in the bedsheets and got out of bed, a little unsteady. Quite a lot unsteady. God, what did I drink last night. My mouth felt like something had slept in it so I looked around for water, anything that was even moist. Nothing. And no bottles or cans in the trash can.

Mini fridge... empty as well.

Have to be the bathroom tap. Yuck.

I knocked on the bathroom door.

"Can I come in and get some water?"

No reply.

"Jo?"

There was a knock on the other door to my right. I practically jumped. Actually I did jump if you count from the waist up while my legs stayed where they were. A most uncomfortable experience when added to the sudden burning sensation of reflux in my oesophagus.

"Oh God, that hurts," I said. "Who the fuck...?"

I looked through the spy hole in door. Nothing and nobody in the corridor. Wait, just at the bottom of my fish-eye vision, the top of someone's head.

"What the...?"

A midget maybe? Sorry, small person. A child?
No, just the night porter bending down to leave
something beside my door.

Maybe it's some water. Anything just so long as it's
wet.

I waited until he had rounded the corner. I didn't
know where I was or how I'd got there but the last
thing I wanted was a conversation with a stranger to
clear things up.

I quietly opened the door into the corridor.

No water. Just a newspaper. I bent over and an
unpleasant woozy, dizzy sensation filled my head as I
picked up the paper.

To hell with reflux, I'm going to be sick. The door to
the bathroom banged against the wall behind it as I
crashed through and dropped to my knees clutching
the toilet. I retched but nothing would come.

I heard the shower curtain pulled back beside me and
felt a sharp pain just above my eye followed by
another blow to the back of my head. Some strange
woman was hitting me harder than you can imagine
possible with one of those long handled shower
brushes you use to reach the parts that smaller
brushes cannot reach.

Before she could find any more parts of my anatomy
with the brush I pushed her back into the shower and
parried her ensuing blows the best I could with an
increasingly soggy rolled up newspaper.

I grabbed the wrist that held the brush.

"Look, I'm sorry but one of us is in the wrong room
and if it's me I'm really sorry but… Good god, it's the

Daily Mail. I'm sorry, it must be me who's in the wrong room because I would never, ever... buy the Daily Mail. Unless...

Chapter Thirty-Three

Play Out

"So not the dream about being menaced by a hooded figure," said Fiona. "That's good."

"Is it?"

"I'm no expert but I would say so. It sounds like a different neurosis."

"And more than one is good, is it?"

"It implies you're a more balanced individual."

"Really?"

"No, I'm just making this up as I go along."

"Very comforting."

"I did ask a shrinky friend for some dream analysis on your hooded figure."

"Shrinky friend?"

"A friend who was a shrink until he got himself unlicensed or whatever for sleeping with his patients."

"Of whom you were one."

"God, no. What would I need a shrink for?"

"So just someone you slept with."

"Yeah. Lousy shrink but a pretty good lay."

"Do I know him?"

"No, this was long before I met you."

"How long?"

"A long time. I was probably sixteen, seventeen at the time."

"And he was?"

"Much, much older. He did consulting work at the school I was attending at the time."

"Your school had a shrink?"

"It was Switzerland. It had everything."

"And you slept with him."

"Once a week for about three months. We did it on his couch."

"Well, of course. Where else? But you didn't think you should see him in his professional capacity."

"No, what for?"

"I don't know… father issues?"

"I never slept with my father."

"But you slept with the much older school psychiatrist."

"Psychiatrist or psychologist. I was never very sure what the difference was."

"About ninety-thousand pounds a year and a prescription pad."

"Probably a psychologist then."

"And you kept in touch?"

"I teach his niece's niece. That's how I got his phone number."

"So what did he say?"

"The first thing he said was he'd like to see me again. I politely declined and told him about your recurring dream."

"And what did Dr Fraud have to say?"

"Mostly waffle, subconscious, unconscious, blah, blah, blah but then he offered a couple of possibilities. One is that you're trying to buy time, to do something or to finish something."

"Sounds like my impending doom fixation. I'm worrying about dying."

"That's what sprung to my mind. And I hadn't told him about your psychic prediction so…"

"So I'm being followed by the grim reaper like I said all along."

"Could be. But it's possible in this scenario the hooded figure might be yourself."

"Not exactly reassuring."

"Sorry."

"What were his other theories?"

"I didn't really get the second one. He said perhaps at some level you think you're being deceived by someone."

"By Dr Fraud, perhaps."

"No, someone close to you."

"Sounds like my family. No surprises there. Could be any one of them."

"I didn't really get everything he said."

"What didn't you get?"

"I didn't see how his theory fitted in with the hooded figure."

"Me neither. Anything else?"

"Maybe you're going to be horribly murdered by a psychopath in a hooded sweatshirt. That's my theory. Horribly literal, I know. I just threw it in for the sake of balance."

"Thanks. Did your shrink friend suggest how I can stop having the dream?"

"He said that some people can resolve a recurring nightmare by going through the dream before you go to sleep only you substitute a happier ending rather than the unpleasant one."

"Might be worth a try."

And try it I did. The next night I was careful to have just one glass of wine with Jo over dinner (Chinese, her choice) with no cheese for afters. I even drank some chamomile tea before getting under the covers. Anything that might help me get a peaceful night's sleep without nightmares. While Jo was brushing her teeth (memo to self: must get Jo her own toothbrush) I went through the recurring nightmare only this time I went with the theory that I was trying to do or complete something or get closure. In my dry run of the dream I turned and faced the mystery figure and pulled down the hood to reveal that the masked figure was in fact myself. I had decided that this nightmare was about my bad habits, namely indecision and procrastination.

Jo wriggled under the covers and as usual used me to warm up her feet, which as usual were like blocks of ice.

"So which dream do you think you'll have tonight then?" Jo asked. "Mr Mystery or the lady in the shower?"

"The first one only I'm hoping for a different ending."

"And this bird in the shower. She wasn't me."

"No."

"Should I be jealous?"

"No. The woman in the shower didn't like me one little bit."

"So not like me at all then."

"No. Not like you. You both have short hair, that's the only thing you had in common."

"Do you like it? You didn't say."

"I think it suits you."

"And the bird in the shower had short hair too?"

"She was blonde whereas… What colour is that by the way?"

"Magenta."

"Actually the woman in the shower looked a bit like Janet Leigh in *Psycho*."

"Never seen it."

"Don't bother. It's overrated. The worst part is the ending. A shrink gives some cod psychiatric explanation of it all. It's a truly terrible scene."

"So you don't want to pretend I'm the bird in the shower while you do me?"

"No. Call me old fashioned, but let's not do that."

I don't know if it was because of Jo's last suggestion or not but it was the the shower dream that began playing in my head before I woke up in terror once more in the middle of the night. Only this time when I looked through the peephole into the corridor it wasn't the night porter I saw. It was the hooded figure.

Chapter Thirty-Four

Playing the Fool

I imagine if you're not 'in the business', if the closest you've ever been to working actors is when you're a member of the audience in a theatre then perhaps they must seem terribly exotic. If you're working at the business end of it, rehearsing a play can in some ways be like any other job.

You have your good days and you have your bad days. But if you work as an accountant you probably have fewer days when you're truly excited by what you do. Those days when, as a director, you see the magic happening right before your eyes. Just a few feet in front of you.

Today had been one of those days. Stuart and Faith were absolutely rocking it. Nailing it. Simply stellar like Nureyev and Fontayne, Burton and Taylor, like Rodgers and Hammerstein. Get the script right and cast it right and there's not much for a director to do. Right?

Right. Some days…

My only contribution had been to tweak a couple of lines here and there but mostly my job had been to stay the hell out of their way and let them go at it. We'd just finished one of the dramatic high points where Stuart's character is trying every tactic possible to get Faith as Judy to stay with him. It was one of the bits I'd had to change to make the new ending work and this was the first time we'd got the scene up on its feet with both actors 'off book'.

There's a reluctance by some actors to learn their lines early in the rehearsal process which frankly amounts to laziness. They will make excuses like they want to explore the part before they learn their lines or say that if they learn the lines too early they will be set in the way they deliver them. It's nonsense as a general rule. They just don't like learning lines and obviously it's easier to learn something you're more familiar with. But you can't act with a script in hand. It's a barrier. You're paying more attention to what's in your grubby little paws than to the other performers onstage.

Good acting is all about re-acting. It's about listening.

"Wow!" I said when Stuart eventually broke out of character because he had dropped a line.

"Wow?"

"Wow!"

"You guys were on fire there."

"Sorry I dropped the line" said Stuart but he was talking to Faith now. "I think maybe I was nervous about the bit coming up."

"We'll get through it together," said Faith. "That's what marriage is all about."

I suddenly realised that was the first time I'd ever heard Faith make a joke, referring to their marital status in the play as if they were a couple in real life.

"Let's break for tea since we've stopped," I said. "We can talk through what comes next if you like, Stuart."

"I'm sure we'll be fine if we just take a run at it," said Stuart.

Sex and violence onstage are difficult for a number of reasons, both for performers and the audience, I think. For the audience there's a danger that sex or violence can break the suspension of disbelief since actors rarely actually hit each other or have actual sexual relations onstage and the audience knows that. Any time an actor takes their clothes off I think the audience immediately starts checking out their physique and I think their engagement with the performance is broken.

For this reason I think kissing onstage is about as far as things should go. Less is more as the saying goes. As an actor myself I've had to kiss people onstage a few times and it's really nothing to get embarrassed about. Since I was never really conventional leading man material I think I have kissed more men onstage than women but that's the way it crumbles, cookie-wise. That was the way my cookie had crumbled at any rate.

So unusually for a straight man in real life I can tell you that it's no fun at all kissing a man with a beard or at least it wasn't any fun for me. In fact my very first professional role in the theatre was to play a gay actor and there was a full on snog with another actor who incidentally was also straight. The only gay person involved in that production was the director who had also written the play. I don't know whether he got off on watching a couple of straight guys kissing because he never commented on that moment in rehearsal. One of my gay friends did give me some feedback though when he came to see it in performance. I asked him if he thought I was convincing as a gay guy and after a moment's hesitation he said "Everything but the kiss."

"What do you mean?" I asked.

"It lacked something. Look like you're enjoying it a little more."

"How do you mean?"

"I don't know. Maybe run your fingers through his hair while you're kissing him."

Perhaps I should have warned the other actor I was about to up the ante the next night because as I did as instructed. The other guys eyes opened wide in what I can only describe as an expression of alarm.

Just as well I didn't slip him the tongue.

Other related and amusing incidents included an actress with whom I had a bit of sexual chemistry offstage. The onstage kisses were getting longer and more passionate with each performance until on the second last show she broke off after the briefest of clinches.

"What's the matter?" I whispered to her offstage.

"I forgot to tell you. My boyfriend's in the audience tonight."

Offstage dramas notwithstanding there's often very little actual passion or chemistry in a stage kiss unless there's real life passion and chemistry between the two actors kissing. Perhaps that's why rumours start about offscreen romances between actors on a film set. It helps sell the film. Sex sells.

The bit we were about to rehearse next in my script was doubly dangerous because it flirted with both sex and violence. It was the culmination of Stuart and Judy fighting and Stuart had fluffed his lines just before Judy was to announce that she was leaving him and taking the kids with her.

New territory for Stuart's character in the play and he had to show vulnerability for the first time which Stuart had actually done really well. What was coming up was the character's desperation at the prospect of his wife and family breaking up before his eyes and I had written the scene so that he grabs his wife and kisses her roughly, having exhausted every other tactic. Not exactly rape within marriage but there was the hint of danger about what might have happened if Judy hadn't been able to break free from him.

I'd actually got the idea for the scene by remembering Corky Oberlander's last throw of the dice in that awful improvisation I'd had to do with Faith at drama school. And now in this play I was actually quite proud of the scene as written. It was more visceral than my usual stuff. A touch of *Cat on a Hot Tin Roof* or *A Streetcar named Desire* I dared to hope with some hints of heat and passion and Williams, Tennessee-ness.

Proud, yes, but a little nervous thinking about Stuart playing it. I didn't have any worries about Faith but Stuart is very controlled as an actor and here he would really have to let go. No safety nets in this three ring circus, not if it was going to fly with an audience.

So I was quite pleased when Stuart didn't want to talk it through over a mug of Tetley's. I thought the more he thinks about it the harder it will be. It's like looking over the edge of a cliff or the top diving board at the swimming pool. Much better just to take a run at it.

What I hadn't factored into the equation was the time of day. Everyone's seen those bloopers and outtakes videos where actors can't stop corpsing over a line. They burst into uncontrollable giggles, sometimes for very little apparent reason. In my experience of rehearsing plays this inevitably takes hold around four in the afternoon if it's going to happen at all. I think it has something to do with the fact that the actors are beginning to tire if they've been at it all day but not so tired that they're close to exhaustion. I read somewhere that there's an ideal temperature for a riot to start. Hot enough for people to want to be outside and start to feel edgy and riotous but not so hot that they simply can't be bothered.

So after two further attempts which got close to the kiss but ended with Stuart the first time and Faith the second going into giggle mode I decided to call it a day for that scene. The last thing I wanted was for Stuart in particular to start getting paranoid over it.

"Maybe we should go back to the part where you slap him, Faith," I said.

"Yes, I think I could really do that with some feeling now."

"Me too," I said.

"Sorry," said Faith. "I could see Stuart was about to go again and that set me off."

"We'll be fine tomorrow," said Stuart. "Maybe it's something we need to work out together. Just the two of us."

"Like over dinner? You and Faith?" I asked. "You turning into a method actor on me, Stu?"

"Maybe over a couple of drinks. loosen up the inhibitions. You free tonight, Faith?"

"No, my other half's had the kids all day and things should be getting close to boiling point around now."

"I hope he's not the jealous kind if he's coming to the show," I said.

"That won't be a problem," Faith said. "He never comes to see me act."

"You're joking," said Stuart.

"No. He hates the theatre. He's seen me in a couple of little telly roles I did when we first met but he's never seen me onstage,"

"Well, he's a fool then," said Stuart. "He doesn't know what he's missing."

Chapter Thirty-Five

Play Innocent

Maybe it just needed a new day or a good night's sleep. Or maybe my theory about four 0'clock being the giggling hour held water. For whatever reason we launched into the scene next morning that had given us trouble the day before and Faith and Stuart aced it. The first run at it was good, the second time they knocked it clean out the ballpark.

"That was great guys," I said. "Absolutely fabulous, darlings. You were marvellous."

I really wasn't much for the "luvvie-darlings, you were marvellous" bit that some theatre folk go in for but on this occasion I was struggling for words to describe what I'd just seen. It had been that good.

"Do we get a 'wow'?" asked Stuart.

"More than one."

"More than one wow?"

"More than one."

"Wow!" said Stuart.

"You're a good writer, Ben," said Faith. "It's a good scene."

"Not that good. I mean, I was pleased with the scene when I wrote it. But that… that was just electric. What you did with it… There was a real danger to it. I felt I didn't know what was going to happen next. What did you think, Jo?"

"Big wow."

"Do you want us to do it again?" asked Stuart.

"No, I don't think so. I don't want to over-rehearse it and kill off whatever energy you two had there. Let's move on."

The next scene involved just me and Faith, so Stuart sat out and watched. It followed on pretty much directly in terms of timeline from the previous scene. Judy was telling Dai that she'd left Stuart and moved in with her mother. What Judy wants is confirmation, reassurance that she's done the right thing and she doesn't want it from her mother.

It was another new scene or rather parts of it were new in order to lead towards the revised ending where Stuart kills Dai and fakes it as a suicide. Directing and acting in the same show obviously has its challenges but I trusted Stuart's instincts as a sort of assistant director as to whether we were moving in the right direction.

"It was good, Ben," Stuart said when we'd finished. "I think what's good about the scene is what's not said. What Dai can't bring himself to say just yet. What he really feels about Judy, that's he's been in love with her from the start."

"That's something I wanted to ask you about, Ben," said Faith. "Do you think Judy's always known that Ben's in love with her?"

"I'm not sure I should answer that."

"How come?" asked Faith.

"Obviously I have an opinion. I wrote it. And because I'm playing Dai I obviously know how he feels about

her. But whether Judy knows or how long she's
known or suspected… I think that's up to you. I think
you should go with your gut feeling."

"I think you should go with whatever feels right,"
said Stuart. "With whatever you're getting from Ben,
sorry Dai."

"It's an entirely fair question," I said. "But I think it's
something only Judy can answer."

"Okay." said Faith.

"So what do you think?" asked Stuart. "Do you think
she knows the poor sap is head over heels in love
with some other guy's wife?"

"That would be telling," said Faith. "On the one hand
she's married to a complete shit but it's a marriage
and I think that's important to her. Did I tell you I
think she's a Catholic."

"Interesting choice," said Stuart. "I like it . The guilt
thing. Are you…?"

"Not practising… Lapsed, but yeah," said Faith. "And
the guilt thing's huge. That's one reason she's at Dai's
now and not talking about it to her mother. I think she
knows Dai well enough to suspect how he feels about
her, but she also knows him well enough to know that
he'd never do anything to break up her marriage to
his oldest friend. So yeah, she might not know how
strong his feelings are but she knows something…
And she's also trying to figure out how she feels
about Dai, but I think if it comes down to it she
knows that if anything's going to happen with her and
Dai that she's got to make the first move."

"She's a smart girl that Judy," said Stuart.

"Smarter than me I think," said Faith.

It was a pretty good piece of analysis and also, I thought, possibly the only time I'd ever heard Faith speak about character or motivation. Usually she didn't talk the talk, she just walked the walk.

"Hey, Ben," said Stuart. "Since we've been sort of spitballing it as it were, why don't we skip a scene for now and do the one where Judy makes the first move on Dai. The moment of truth, the big kiss. You haven't done that one off book yet."

"I don't know. What do you think, Faith?"

"I brushed my teeth this morning so I'm game if you are." The second time I'd heard Faith make a joke. Curious…

Curious? I guess I was.

I'd written the scene where Judy and Dai eventually kiss for the first time as a delicious will they, won't they thing. At least that's what I hoped. I wanted the audience, who hopefully had been rooting for Dai all along, to have this fleeting Hollywood happy ending bit before saying to themselves - wait a minute, the nice guy's got the girl but we know from the first scene that Dai's dead… that he's committed suicide. So what the hell…?

It was a tightrope I was hoping would play until the last scene when it would slowly dawn on the audience what's actually going to happen. That one best friend will kill another because he can't stand losing the girl. There's nothing more fatal for an actor to start thinking this is going well. Usually it happens in performance in the middle of a run when you relax or let yourself get distracted and it usually happens to me when the words "this is going rather well , isn't it" come into my mind. That's when you'll suddenly drop a line or worse still dry, meaning you'll completely forget what you're supposed to say next. You literally dry up. Maybe the expression comes from the feeling of dry mouth that might hit you at that moment. And usually it happens in a place where you least expect it, where you've always been word perfect. Which I usually am. I hardly ever dry or drop a line.

In my experience it happens less often in rehearsal but that's what happened here. The scene was going really well. Dai can't bring himself to tell Judy how he feels about her even though she's obviously opening the door for him, as it were, to say it. So no acting required on my part you'd think given my past history with Faith. And yes, I thought, this is going swimmingly, right up to the point where Judy despairs of Dai having the courage to speak up and instead she kisses him. A long, lingering, much longed for kiss.

"Wow," was what I thought and might have said if my lips hadn't been busy. What a kiss, a kiss to end all kisses… but she's just acting right, she's just being Faith, being a good actress. So no, she's not being Faith, she's being Judy, only it being Faith she's totally one hundred per cent Judy in love with Dai when she's wasted half a lifetime being with someone else. This jumble of thoughts was what was going through my head instead of my being inside Dai's head. If I'd been in a Victorian melodrama I might have swooned and fainted.

"Okay," I said after clearing my throat and getting my breath back. "Let's move on… unless you had something to say, Stuart?"

"You've got a line, stupid."

"Sorry?"

"The last line in the scene. You're supposed to say 'What about Stuart?'

"Sorry, I forgot. Sorry, Faith."

"No biggie," said Faith. "No problem. We nearly got there."

Chapter Thirty-Six

Play with Fire

Getting slapped onstage is fine and if you both get your timing right nobody actually gets slapped. In real life things are a little more messy and somehow Jo managed to connect with my ear and my right eye and even my nose in quick succession leaving me with a ringing sound, a twitching eyelid and a runny nose when she slapped me hard across the face.
"What the..?"
"You fucking bastard. You lying, fucking bastard."
Faith and Stuart had already left in a hurry. Faith because she had to rescue her kids and Stuart because he had some thing to get to. I hadn't asked what because I'd seen the expression on Jo's face and pretty much knew that something was about to kick off. But I'd expected words, maybe some yelling but not a slap in the face. Maybe Stuart and Faith had sensed an eruption too and that's why they'd hurried off.
"You said you didn't love her."
"I don't."
"Then why the fuck did you drop the line? Cat got your tongue? Or was it Faith?"
"It was just a stage kiss. Just acting."
"Bullshit. Even Stuart saw it. You should have seen the expression on his face."

"People drop lines all the time."

"Not you. You don't. Not to mention you wrote the bloody thing."

Jo was jamming her things into her shoulder bag like someone trying to strangle a turkey with one hand and stuff it with the other all in one go.

"You weren't just swapping spit. That was a fucking chemistry experiment," Jo said.

"So what are we we doing here? Are we breaking up? Over two characters kissing in a play?"

"It was a lot more than that, Ben. We both know it was a lot more than that."

"So what are you saying?"

"I'm saying I'm about to catch the next bus home. But I'll be back in time to set up for rehearsal first thing Monday morning. I'm a fucking professional, not some emotional teenager with a crush."

"I take it you mean me. So what are we? Just friends? Fuck buddies who've had a fight? What?"

"I'll have to think about the fuck part. We're not fucking buddies. I'll tell you that for nothing."

Funny how a day can start off so well and finish kind of crappy.

Chapter Thirty-Seven
Play it by Ear

One of the fastest break ups in history, I think you'll agree, in terms of fight time. I hadn't put a clock on it but it was surely all over in the first round. I was left temporarily deaf in one ear and wondering what future Jo's parting shot left open. The possibility of a resumption in intimacies or possibly hostilities in the near future. Unsure about this and what I should do next, I went to ask Fiona's advice.

"Tell me again. How did she leave it? What were her exact words?" asked Fiona.

"Not fucking buddies. Not just now. Something along those lines."

"I'd say that maybe things aren't over and maybe that your little fuck buddy likes you a little more than she's been letting on."

"That sounds like ominous."

"That sounds like an apology is in order."

"What do I have to apologise for?"

"Oh Ben, where should I start?"

"It was just a stage kiss. Two actors kissing. It's in the script. What was I supposed to do?"

"Are you sure that's all it was?"

A moment's hesitation on my part before answering...

"No..."

"I think you've got to work out how you feel about Jo. But first of all you've got to figure out what it is you feel for Faith."

"Talk about feelings when I'm stone cold sober?"

"Look on it as one small step for man, one giant leap for mankind."

"A man. Neil Armstrong said 'a man' but it got lost in transmission."

"Stop being evasive."

"Actually his first words on the moon were 'what a craphole.' but mission control thought that lacked resonance."

"Ben…"

"Not to mention grandeur."

"She should have hit you harder. Not a mistake that I'm about to make if you don't stop doing what you always do which is to avoid facing facts."

"What was the question again?… Ow that hurt."

I was relieved that she'd poked me in the ribs rather than slapped me. Fiona was a good deal stronger than Jo and had very long levers.

"The question was twofold but surprisingly simple. What do you feel about Jo and what do you feel about Faith?"

"I think I'd prefer another blow to the head." I flinched under the threat of another impact. This time it was a cushion in the face.

"Okay, okay," I said and took a deep breath. "I think that what I feel about Jo is… I thought we were just having a bit of fun and that's all there was to it."

"There's almost always more to it."

212

"I haven't cheated on her."

"You're in love with someone else or at least that's what Jo thinks and that's far worse."

"Really?"

"Potentially more fatal."

"For me?"

"For you and Jo."

"I see."

"Do you?"

"Yes and no."

"Which is it?"

"I see but don't understand."

"Don't understand? Confused, you are, young Jedi."

"Yes... fucked am I."

"Use the force."

"The force?"

"Your feelings. What do you feel in your gut. In your fingers? In your toes?"

"That love is all around us?"

"So let the feeling grow... What do you feel about Faith?"

"It doesn't matter what I feel about Faith."

"It does to Jo."

"Yes, she made that painfully clear."

"And it matters to you too."

"I feel... I think... I think Faith's adorable but I don't think I'm... I was just fine until she kissed me."

"Which means?"

"That she's a good kisser or she's a great actress. How the fuck should I know?"

"You could ask her."

"I don't need to ask her. She's married."

"Happily?"

"As far as I know."

"And is that far enough?"

"Yes, I think so. Faith's not available. So in the end it doesn't matter how or what I feel. It's totally irrelevant."

"Not to Jo."

"Apparently not."

"It's also a massive rationalisation. A great big juicy one."

"What?"

"That she's not available so it doesn't matter how you feel. It clearly matters to you otherwise what the hell are we talking about?"

"Damned if I know."

"And damned if you don't it would seem."

"A paradox it is, Master Yoda."

"So what's the plan, Ben?"

"Carry on where we left off. Jo said she was going to be a professional and on time for Monday's rehearsal and I'm going to do the same. Maybe I can use it in performance with Dai. This whole… whatever. That's my plan."

"That's not much of a plan. In fact, it's not so much a plan as another of your juicy rationalisations."

"It'll have to do for now because that's all I've got."

"If you can't face getting everything out in the open I think you should try to put Faith out of your mind. Just think of her as Judy. Be professional about it, like you said. That will have to do for now. You've all still got to work together. You got a show to do."

"And Jo?"

"I think a grovelling apology is on order."

"Really?"

"I'm just looking at that bloodshot eye of yours. It's not attractive. God help you if you're single again."

Chapter Thirty-Eight

Play it Cool

Where grown men are concerned there are two things that should be kept from public gaze. Lycra shorts and grovelling apologies. Jo wasn't the sort that could be assuaged with flowers and an apologetic note. For one thing she had chronic hay fever and asthma though when her inhaler had appeared twice in bed I took it not as a sign of danger but as a signal I was doing well.

Now did not seem the right time for an ill-judged joke which was my go to setting in most socially awkward situations and that remained my feeling all the way through Saturday and most of Sunday, By the time my little red car pulled up outside Jo's flat I was relieved to find Jo had cooled off some and we managed to have something approaching an adult conversation about how things stood between us.. Whether my apology was sufficiently grovelling I can't say for sure, but after an hour we'd come to some sort of truce and a begrudging agreement on her part that no promises had been exchanged between us and at worst I had been guilty of a thought crime. I hadn't actually been unfaithful if you'll pardon the pun. I didn't point it out to Jo. Un-Faith-ful. Now was not the right time to draw Jo's attention to the comedy potential of the moment.

And that's how we left it. If I'd stayed longer or we'd had a drink together we might even have had break-up-make-up sex but as much fun as we'd had together in the sack… well, not to put too fine a point on it, that's mostly what it had been. Fun in the sack. And I for one wasn't sure yet whether we should go back to that or not. Because once the ringing in my ear had stopped, for which I was grateful, I was clear headed enough to realise that there was more to life than sack races or a race to the sack and more to life was exactly what I wanted.

Right now we had a show to do and ten days left before opening night. And the show, as everybody knows, must go on. And on we got, even if we didn't all get on quite as before. Jo was at least true to her word and utterly professional and I tried to be the same. And after our first day back on Monday, when it was if there was a lingering bad smell in the air, things just about got back to normal, normal being turn up on time, know your lines and don't think about shagging the stage manager. Or anyone else. The atmosphere got a little frosty when we broke for lunch or tea but everyone seemed to find some comfort in just getting on with the work.

And doing it well. Stuart and Faith continued to walk on air as it were and if I was afraid of being somewhat earth bound by comparison they both reassured me that all was well and it was actually no bad thing if Dai seemed to have something of a cloud around him.

And so on we marched even if we were less a band of brothers, more a band where the lead guitarist is no longer speaking to the drummer. Ten days to go became three and, as usually happens, the approach of opening night brought us closer together as a team even though Jo still bolted for the bus stop within seconds of us finishing at the end of the day and Stuart had by now started giving Faith a ride home, which was nice of him and helped her out marginally, I assumed, with her child care issues. Her part of west London was not one well served by public transport and her journey home otherwise involved three changes and trains both underground and mainline. This all left me at a bit of a loose end at the end of the day. I got into the habit of having one pint of Guinness alone to unwind at the local watering hole before going home for something to eat. The last thing I needed was to hit the bottle in production week, no matter how tempting that might have been.

Chapter Thirty-Nine

Play On

We moved into the theatre and the technical rehearsal went well with us doing a stop-start run to let Jo go through all the lighting and sound cues. She knew more about how to get a particular lighting state onstage than I did so it quickly became our practice that I briefly said what I wanted and she and the tech guy from the theatre adjusted the lighting rig. All that was required then was to fine tune the lighting levels and programme each lighting state into the lighting-desk-computer-box thingy and no I didn't know how to do that either.

"I am an artiste," I said jokingly to the theatre's technician.

"Oh yeah, we get a lot of those," he replied, rolling his eyes.

"A piss-artiste," Jo added in passing.

I decided that mockery based in truth was better than being bitch-slapped by your girlfriend. Ex-girlfriend, lover whatever it was we were or used to be.

Whether it was because this was Jo's big day as stage manager or there had been a sufficiently long cooling off period, I don't know, but Jo even managed the occasional smile when we got each lighting state as we wanted it.

"Right on!" she would say each time, a strangely American hippie expression for a sarf' London girl but a favourite of Jo's and one that I had previously found a little annoying. Now I was grateful to hear it again and hoped it might signal an improvement in relations.

Technical rehearsals can be notoriously hard work and invariably run late into the night but ours was a relatively straight forward affair with no difficult scene changes or technical effects required. This was just a little three hander after all. We weren't talking *Les Miserables.* The day went smoothly and we finished around 7pm.

"I'm going for a burger and a pint if anyone wants to join me," I said.

Nobody did and everyone made polite protestations of childcare commitments or needing an early night but Jo kissed me on the cheek before saying "maybe tomorrow" which I took to be a further step towards improving relations. I assumed she meant going to to the pub rather than anything else but I think I caught Faith smiling out of the corner of my eye and Stuart winked at me on the way out with a "go get em', cowboy" remark that I thought was uncalled for and unnecessary and therefore entirely in character.

But in spite of these good wishes I felt quite, quite alone that night as I watched Stuart opening the car door for Faith before giving her a ride home. I found myself wondering what they talked about on the journey across London to her house.

"See you tomorrow, sport," he said with a cheerful salute as he got in behind the wheel. It was a form of address which he knew annoyed me and he usually only employed it when he was in full roister doister mode. Ralph Roister Doister is the eponymous lead character in what is thought to be the first comedy ever written for the English stage. It pre-dates Shakespeare by several decades and Stuart had been in line to play the title role in a profit share production that never got off the ground. No funding, let alone production or profit.

Stuart had grown a rakish moustache before the start of rehearsals that never were and had been planning on channelling his inner Errol Flynn into his interpretation of the role. And he took to calling me 'sport' for a while, an affectation once apparently used liberally by the Australian trouser snake and one time movie star. Stuart had been using it a lot again lately to annoy me since I gently but firmly turned down his suggestion to let him grow a pencil moustache for his part in my play. I'd suggested he keep the Terry-Thomas act for the golf course.

"And I'll bet you won't let me do it with a limp and a stutter either," he'd said at the time. An old acting joke.

"You'll just have to try acting, Stuart."

"Screw that."

I think we'd probably had a conversation something along those lines every time we performed together.

I saw the brake lights of Stuart's car light up. He stopped the car and backed up until he was level with me once more. He lowered the driver's window.

"Hey, Ben. The show's going to be great. Don't worry."

Then Faith chipped in. "Ben, don't go to the pub on your own."

"Why don't you just go home and get a couple of beers from the supermarket?" Stuart said.

"Okay, sport," I said, attempting a cheery salute.

And I took his advice. A four pack of Guinness, of which I had two, and a delivery pizza. I watched *Casablanca* for the umpteenth time which you probably know is about, well it's about a lot of things, it's that good a film, but it concerns a woman who finds herself torn between two men both of whom she loves in different ways. I'd never before made the possible connection between the film and my play. It certainly wasn't in my head when I wrote it, at least as far as I was aware.

Famously Ingrid Bergman didn't know which of the two men in the film she would choose to go with because the final scene of the screenplay hadn't been written when they started filming. Something which probably only added to her performance. As usual I was transfixed by her beauty and her apparently effortless performance and, as always, I had to fight back the tears during the singing of *La Marseillaise* and Bogey's unpolished pearl of wisdom.

"It doesn't take much to see that the problems of three little people don't amount to a hill of beans in this crazy world. Someday you'll understand that."

The problems of three little people... Boy, could I relate to that and oh boy, was it a bad idea to watch this particular movie when I should be getting a good night's sleep. I closed my eyes and tried not to think about how much Faith looked like Ingrid Bergman.

* * * *

With the technical rehearsal completed on schedule, which doesn't always happen by any means, we had time for two dress rehearsals the next day if we wanted to do it twice. Costumes were pretty straight forward as they came straight from the actors' wardrobes. I've always hated stage make up and never been very good at it so I usually ask someone to do it for me. In this case Faith volunteered and it was pretty much a case of a little powder to take off the sheen under the lights and a little highlighting of my otherwise unremarkable features. I tried not to notice how nice she smelt. Clean, freshly washed. Yes, I tried hard not to notice that.

Stuart had been more restrained than usual when it came to flirting with the make up lady, given who it was in this case. It didn't stop the inevitable repetition of his usual advice to anyone doing my make up for me which involved, among other things, bursting into a chorus of *The Phantom of the Opera* and a line from *The Elephant Man*.

"I am not an animal! I am a human being!"

"Practising for your next stage role, Stuart? The Elephant Man?" I asked.

"Hey, I'm not the one who could do it without make-up."

"Stop squabbling you two. Save it for the performance," Faith said.

Stuart and I complied but not before Stuart added "I am not… an elephant…" quietly as if it was part of his vocal warm up and I had countered with "no, an elephant would never forget his lines in the last scene".

On the plus side, this friendly banter implied we were all fairly relaxed with a day to go before our first public performance. I read once that the nerves or stress experienced by some actors before going onstage is comparable to someone about to drive a car over a cliff or something like that, though God knows how they managed to measure that. Apparently Daniel Day Lewis had a nervous breakdown playing Hamlet because he used to have visions of his own dead father in the ghost scenes.

Hey diddly dee, an actor's life for me… I have heard actors throw up in the toilet before a first night which made me wonder why they did it. I became an actor partly because I was happier being someone other than myself but also because it was fun. Being happier pretending to be another person was one of the things that emboldened me to apply for drama school. It's something that Stanislavsky says about himself and many other actors in one of his books. I forget which one and I don't recommend you bother reading them all to find out. They're pretty dry stuff and they won't turn you into the next Marlon Brando. Or Daniel Day Lewis. Our first and, as it turned out only, dress rehearsal went as well you could expect for a dress rehearsal. Nobody died and nobody saw their dead father.

There's a theatrical superstition that a disastrous dress rehearsal means you'll have a great opening night. I've never heard of anyone saying the converse might be true but I decided not to tempt fate by having a second dress rehearsal and sent everyone home early. Everyone joined me in the pub for one drink because of the early finish or maybe it was to make sure I kept to my one or two pints only protocol.

Usually everyone's exhausted after two days of technical and dress rehearsals and gets through the first public performance on adrenaline and not much else. But we were all going to be back for the first performance well rested and relaxed on the 'morrow. One reason for this might have been that our first public performance was billed as a preview rather than an official opening night. This meant we would be performing mainly for a friendly audience made up of well, friends, and a few members of the public whom we asked to make only a donation which we would give to charity, an actor's benevolent fund. So there would be nobody potentially hostile or overly judgemental. And no newspaper reviewers. So maybe that's why we were all fairly relaxed and as confident

as we could be that the preview performance would
go well the next day.
Which it did.

Chapter Forty

Opening Play

I'd started taking a sleeping tablet in the last few days of production week. I'd tried taking them in the past without much effect but Fiona had given me some of her prescription ones which pretty much knocked me out for eight hours and if I woke up as I sometimes still did in a cold sweat from a bad dream, I could towel dry and be asleep again within a short time. Opening night proper went like clockwork until I dried completely in Act Two. I knew I had a cue line for Stuart to come onstage but I just stood there sweating under the lights suffering what felt like a panic attack.

There in the third row was the hooded figure as clear as, well not clear as day but clear as I could see while blinking with sweat pouring into my eyes. The same grey hooded sweatshirt, sat in the dark, the face mostly in shadow under the prominent peak of a hip-hop-type baseball cap. For one second I thought it might have been my brother's face but he wouldn't have been seen dead in a baseball cap of any variety. Wicked? Yes. Gangsta'? Not so much.

Fortunately for the performance my fear and discomfort was in keeping with that moment in the play and eventually I stumbled my way through the cue line. And fortunately for me what followed shortly after was a scene between Stuart and Faith so I had some time to pull myself together and when I came back onstage I glanced towards the third row and there was just an empty seat.

I made it somewhat shakily through the rest of the performance and as the lights came on for the curtain call I could confirm that whoever or whatever I'd seen wasn't in the audience if indeed they ever had been.

The applause that greeted us confirmed my feeling that, my dodgy second half performance apart, the first night had gone well and I declined to share the truth about my encounter, vision, apparition or whatever it had been with the rest of the cast as we sat round a table for a drink in the pub.

"What was up with you when you were late with my cue in Act Two?" Stuart asked. "You looked like you'd seen a ghost."

"Nothing… I think I was just having a Daniel Day Lewis moment. No, the last few nights I've been taking sleeping tablets that Fiona gave me. Think they've got some side effects."

"Then stop taking them," said Faith. " The show went great. You've got nothing to worry about."

The show going great was the gist of the newspaper review we woke up to next day. It said some nice things about me as the playwright but what the reviewer reserved her five star praise for was Stuart and Faith's onstage chemistry. "Sizzling, hot, passionate", not terms I had linked with Stuart on stage before. There was even mention of a modern

Tennessee Williams that I was quietly chuffed about though I think that might have had something to do with the lack of air conditioning in the theatre. Advance bookings had been fairly sparse for the rest of our three week run at the theatre but that quickly changed thanks to this and two other rave reviews from the first night. We began to sell out days in advance as further positive notices appeared in the press. Friends and old acquaintances from drama school began ringing up out of the blue. Everyone likes to be associated with a hit, especially actors if there's even the remotest chance of the new hit playwright having another show casting in the near future. So we suddenly went from being 'what's it called, never heard of it, written by who, where the hell is that, is that in London? I didn't know there was a theatre there,' to being as close as you can get to the must see show in a small fringe theatre kind of way. The pub downstairs were of course delighted with this steady stream of new customers and we became minor celebrities there too if you count just having to nod to the barman to order a round of drinks for the cast. One night we even got an "it's on the house" round of drinks which is pretty much unheard of in London.

Somewhere into the second week I came into the pub at the same time as Faith and Jo after the show to see Stuart talking to a group of guys, one of whom I recognised as someone I'd played cricket with once for the Stage Cricket Club.

"Here he is, the man of the hour," Stuart said beckoning me over.

"Do you want me to get you a drink from the bar, Ben?" Faith asked.

"Yes, please. Guinness. You're an angel."

"I'll give you a hand," said Jo.

I thought I noticed an almost imperceptible narrowing of the eyes from Jo and immediately regretted what I'd said but there was no time to take it back and Faith and Jo squeezed their way through the crowd on their way to the bar.

"Do you remember, Mike?" Stuart asked. "He's gone over to the enemy now. Plays for London Theatres." It turned out that half their regular team had come out to see the show, so I thanked them for that and made polite protestations about not playing cricket any more, far too old, what with these knees? That kind of thing. I tried to swallow and get some saliva going as the pub was pretty much packed to capacity and roasting hot in a way only a London pub with negligible air conditioning can be.

I looked over towards the bar in the hope of a drink coming my way but I couldn't see Faith. Then I caught sight of the top of Jo's magenta coloured head making her way over in our direction holding a Bacardi freezer to her chest and a pint of Guinness aloft like a diminutive punk rock version of the Statue of Liberty.

"Thanks, Jo. You're a life saver."

I nearly said 'angel' but stopped myself in time.

Fortunately Stuart made the introductions for Jo as the new arrival to the group. I'd forgotten most of the names on the team sheet, as it were.

"Jo thinks cricketers are boring," I said.

"Not when they look like this one," she said stroking the arm of the youngest guy in the group. "You're gorgeous. What did you say your name was?"

"Paul," said the young, gorgeous one.

"But he also answers to Gorgeous," said Mike.

"I'm not surprised," said Jo. "So what do you do, Gorgeous Paul."

"I'm an actor. We're all actors apart from Mike. He's a director."

"No, I mean what do you do, like, are you one of the batters or one of the fielder blokes."

"I'm a bowler."

"Pretty fast too. But he's being modest. He can give the ball a bit of a belt too," said Mike.

"I'll bet he can," said Jo. "Must be why you got all them muscles," Jo said, giving his arm a squeeze just to make sure. "I like fast men."

"Thanks," said Paul. "You're pretty fast yourself."

Not a bad comeback I thought for someone who wasn't sure if this was his lucky night or he was being set up for a fall.

"Where's Faith?" said Stuart. "I'm supposed to be her ride home tonight."

"Make sure you just have the one pint then," I said.

"She's over there in the corner," said Jo. "Talking to that massive bloke with the shoulders."

"Bloody hell!" said Stuart. "Who's that gorilla? Did the pub get a new bouncer?"

"That's James, her husband." said Mike. "He came to see the show. Said he'd never seen his Mrs onstage."

"Doesn't look like he enjoyed the experience much," said Stuart. "How do you know him?"

"He's our new ringer," said Mike. "Used to be a pro. Played a couple of seasons for Middlesex before he started having back trouble. Only bowls off a few paces these days, but he's still quicker than anything I've ever seen."

"Now that you mention it, he does look kind of familiar," said Stuart.

"So is he better than you, Paulie?" Jo asked.

"No comparison. I don't even come close."

"You can't compare amateurs with pro's," said Stuart. "It's like a different game."

"I'm not comparing him. I like what I've got right here, don't I, Paul… So if he's so much better how come he plays with you lot? Don't sound fair."

"Got to play for someone. Lot of the amateur teams have a ringer," said Mike. Usually a young Australian bloke or a South African over here looking for experience. Sort of backpackers with a bat. But old Jamesie usually puts them in their place. He wouldn't try to hurt any sh-amateurs like us and we only play friendlies, not league stuff. But he always sniffs out the ringer in their side. The accent usually gives them away of course. Plus you can tell after a couple of balls the ones that can really play. And if they can keep James out then believe you me, they can play."

232

The crowd in the pub always seems to part if you're a bloke James' size and it was a bit like Moses and the Red Sea as he made his way over to us with Faith a couple of steps behind.

"So you're the bloke my Mrs went to drama school with, are you?" he asked, looking down at me from a considerable height.

I'd like to say I was brave like the philosopher who met Alexander the Great and merely asked him to step aside as he was blocking the sunlight. At close quarters this bloke looked like he could cause a solar eclipse and I've always been unnerved meeting people much bigger than myself. I always felt like Charlie Chaplin, dwarfed by the villain, but there was no danger of me ever being brave enough to kick them in the pants.

"Yes, that's me…. I'm Ben. Nice to meet you. James is it?" I reached out a hand and predictably his enveloped mine and just as predictably crushed it for a little longer than I felt was strictly necessary.

"And this is the passion wagon I've been reading about in the papers."

"I'm Stuart. Nice to meet you."

Something about the look on James' face must have told Stuart that a handshake was not in the offing. Stuart's hand twitched momentarily but he covered it by moving his pint into his right hand.

"Fancy a drink or are you driving?" asked Stuart. "Jim, was it?"

"James… No, we've got an Uber coming for us and the lads. Minivan. Mate of mine. Should be here any minute. Thought I'd do him a favour. Put a nice little fare his way. I hear you're a cricketer, Stuart."

"Now and again."

"Stuart still plays for the Stage," said Mike.

"We've already played them, haven't we lads? Few weeks back was it? Don't remember seeing you there... Stuart." James' almost imperceptible pause seemed to carry with it a continued air of menace but Stuart ignored it.

"We were rehearsing. Couldn't make it for a midweek game."

"Pity. Do you play?" He turned to me and I caught a whiff of bad breath. Or perhaps that's what an excess of testosterone smells like at close quarters.

"Me, no. Not in a long time."

"We're playing an Authors XI at the weekend, Ben. And they're short a couple of players. I know because their skipper rang me to see if I could think of anyone." It was Mike again, trying to be helpful as always but I wished he'd just shut up.

"Performing. Can't, sorry." I shrugged my shoulders, hoping that would seal or rather cancel any possible deal being negotiated.

"Not on Sunday you're not," said James. "Faith's bringing the ankle biters along for a picnic."

"I don't think I've got any kit that would fit me anymore."

"You can borrow some of mine, Ben," said Mike. "We're pretty much the same shape, you and me these days. Everything but the jock strap but I'm sure your old one will stretch to the occasion."

"That's it settled then," said Stuart, refusing to make eye contact with me. "Call the skipper and tell him we'll be there. Where is there by the way?"

"Bank of England ground. One o'clock. The Bank's home fixture got cancelled and I called up a favour from an old team mate and asked if we could use their ground," said James.

"You know, I think I saw you play a one day game against Surrey at the Oval," said Stuart. "Before you got injured. Your back wasn't it? What was it? A spinal thing?"

"Stress fracture." James took out his phone. "That's our Uber, hun," he said to Faith. "Let's go. Coming, lads?"

James took Faith by the hand and led her towards the door. I suddenly realised she hadn't said a word.

"I think I'll get a night bus later," said Paul.

"See you Sunday, Paul?" asked Mike.

"Not sure whether I can make it on Sunday. I'll give you a call." He went back to chatting up Jo who by now I suspected might be the reason for Paul's possible unavailability.

"Well, I'll see you two fellows on Sunday, right?" said Mike. "Don't forget your jock strap, Ben."

He followed his teammates out the door.

"Jesus, Stuart," I said quietly. "What the fuck? For a second I thought he was going to pull out a gun, not a mobile phone."

"The encounter did have a certain gunslinger quality, didn't it?"

"What the hell have you dragged me into?"

"Don't worry about him. It's probably all gym muscle."

"Which means, for one thing, he goes to a gym. The man played professionally for Christ's sake."

"Sprayed the ball around like a fire hose. I remember him now. There was no telling where the ball was going to go. Mostly to the boundary for four or six off the middle of Alec Stewart's bat if memory serves."

"Would this have been Alec Stewart's Captain of England phase or his opening the batting for England phase?"

"I don't recall. Possibly both."

Chapter Forty-One

Play Fast Ball

There's a breathless hush in the close to-night
Ten to make and the match to win
A bumping pitch and a blinding light,
An hour to play, and the last man in.
And it's not for the sake of a ribboned coat.
Or the selfish hope of a season's fame,
But his captain's hand on his shoulder smote
"Play up! Play up! And play the game!

This wasn't quite the scene at the Bank of England
Cricket Cub. The facilities as you might imagine are
pretty amazing for a club ground. Not just your
average village green. I think the ground had been the
venue for a few first class games some years before
so a bumping pitch was unlikely. A blinding light
there was, however, as I arrived at 12.30.
There were no ribboned coats as far as the eye could
see I but straight away I spotted Stuart who was
already there and changed. You could scarcely miss
him as he invariably wore a spectacular though moth
eaten cricket cap with contrasting colours in four
quadrants. Spectacular if your taste in clothes could
be described as harlequinesque or clownish. He once
claimed it belonged to his grandfather but I wasn't
sure I believed him because he was evasive when

asked whose club colours he was wearing into battle. He always wore it at a slightly jaunty angle, carefully calculated to annoy his opponents to a maximum degree.

"Look who I brought with me," he said beckoning me to come over.

The man in the umpire's coat next to Stuart turned towards me and I saw that it was Charles Collingwood, former captain of the Stage Cricket Club and a very lovely man, blessed with old school charm and a slightly camp sense of humour. Stuart liked to refer to him as Charles Charley Charles after a character in a Harry Enfield comedy sketch but never to his face. Charles had enjoyed far more success than Stuart or I as an actor. He and his wife had been on The Archers for years together. Talk about taking your work home with you.

Charles was always regarded with great affection and respect by his team mates and it was clear that as a young man he'd been better than all of us put together. Any time I thought about taking up cricket again I knew that without Charles as club captain it wouldn't be half so much fun. He was also a natural leader which probably had nothing to do with the fact that his ancestor, Admiral Collingwood, had won the Battle of Trafalgar in 1805. And don't tell me it was Nelson because he was lying mortally wounded below decks and cosy-ing up to Captain Hardy when the battle was won.

"Not playing today, Charles?" I asked.

"No, Ben. My flannels are strictly on gardening duty these days. I just came along because Stuart invited me to umpire. And they do a smashing tea here. Lovely strawberry tart."

"Yes, I think I remember from playing here once before."

"Think you got a few runs that day, didn't you, Ben?"

"A few. Very slowly as usual. Mostly I remember some Australian kid who hit the ball like a shell. I remember standing at extra cover, quietly terrified."

"Yes," said Charles. "And he was called Vaughan Williams, I remember. Like the composer."

"Mostly I remember being really happy to see he was a wicket keeper and not a bowler when we were batting."

"I've heard the opposition's got someone pretty lively today."

"Yes, we know his wife," I said.

"Not in the biblical sense, I hope," Charles said.

"Charles has come to see fair play," said Stuart. "I've made him promise to make sure he's standing at James' end if he's opening the bowling."

"Which I think is a pretty safe assumption," I said.

"How will I know which one he is?" said Charles.

"You'll know." Stuart and I both spoke together.

"What are you? Some sort of comedy double act these days?" asked Charles.

"I'm just hoping it's a comedy today and not a tragedy," I said. "I haven't held a bat since I last played for you."

"Gosh, that was a long time ago," Charles said. "I'm sure it will all come back to you. Best of luck. I think I smelt coffee brewing. I'll see you both out on the field of battle."

I was happy to see Charles again and even happier that he was umpiring. But I couldn't help wondering whether Stuart's invitation to Charles didn't slightly undermine his apparent nonchalance about facing James, the giant, with a cricket ball in his enormous paw rather than something soft like a big peach. It was a nonchalance that in retrospect had been increasingly forced and less convincing with each passing day.

"Don't worry, old sport. We can handle him." Stuart had said that more than once and I wondered which one of us he was trying to convince. I tried not to think about the statistic I once read that, in the professional game, a batsman sometimes had the equivalent time of the blink of an eye between the ball being released and it hitting the bat. That was assuming it hit his bat and not some part of his anatomy.

Stuart and I were about to go and look at the pitch when we saw the two captains going out to the middle to toss up so we wandered over to the pavilion. The sight of James taking his shirt off through an open door did nothing to reassure me but did at least tell us that our team was using the smaller, Away Team's dressing room. I quickly changed into the kit Mike had lent me. I had made sure that the loan included a helmet which had what looked like a reassuring amount of ironwork by way of a protective grill. I'd already tried it on and adjusted it to fit at home in front of the mirror. More than once.

Our team captain returned and announced he'd won the toss and we were going to bowl first. He came over to introduce himself. He already knew Stuart from a previous encounter.

"Roger Barratt, nice to meet you" he said to me.

"What do you do, Ben? Bat or bowl?"

"I don't generally bowl unless you want to lose the game."

"That's a pity. We're a bit short on bowlers which is why I put them in. Never mind, we'll just have to see how many they get and then try to chase it down. So you're a batsman, are you?"

"After a fashion."

"Ben's more of your stonewall type than your dasher but he's got a forward defensive that would bring a tear to Geoffrey Boycott's eye," said Stuart.

"Might get you to go in first up then. We're missing one of our usual openers. His wife is expecting."

"Errr… " I said.

"Or first drop. Send you in at three to steady the ship if need be. Have a think and let me know where you'd like to bat at tea since you're making a guest appearance. Your choice."

Hobson's choice, I thought.

"Thanks for coming out by the way. I should have started with that, shouldn't I. Where's my manners? Stuart, you might need to turn your arm over and I'll probably have you bat at four if that's okay with you with me at five and Boom-Boom at six. You can maybe give it a biff once Ben's worn them down a bit.You know Boom-Boom, don't you? I was going to try the young boy warming up out there as opener today but they've got a pretty ferocious bowling attack, I hear."

Roger Barratt fetched a new ball out of his bag and went outside to do a fairly leisurely warm up. Boom-Boom said hello to Stuart and shook me by the hand before following Roger out with the rest of the team leaving me and Stuart momentarily alone.

"Boom-Boom?" I asked Stuart

"Nickname. You'll see why when he bats. Or fields."

I dragged myself to my feet and walked out into the sunshine that seemed to be even brighter and hotter than before.

"No chance of rain at all," I thought. "Buggery, buggering, bugger it…" I said under my breath.

Roger opened the bowling at one end with the young boy who turned out to be his son bowling the first over at the other end. Ryan, the youngster, was tall and thin with a whippy action. His first ball was short of a length and their opening bat, ginger haired and chunky, tonked him over square leg for a one bounce four. The kid's third ball surprised him with extra pace and he edged it to Boom-Boom in the gully. Roger bowled left arm over the wicket at a more leisurely pace but managed to find a prodigious amount of inswing which surprised their other opener first ball and clean bowled him. That wicket brought their captain to face and he clearly looked like he could play. He crashed his first ball through the covers for four and clipped the next ball wide of mid on for another boundary. Roger's last ball in the over was another big in swinger which the batsmen lofted in the direction of fine leg only to find Boom-Boom, positioned there by Roger in what looked like a brilliant piece of intuition. He took another fine catch high and to his left. Pretty impressive for someone who looked a few years older than me.

Stuart was fielding at cover point to my left.

"Boom-Boom's part man, part rubber ball," he said.

"So I see. At this rate we might skittle them out and be home by tea…" Without me having to bat, I was thinking. Thinking and hoping and hoping and thinking…

"Look who's in next." Stuart said.

James was striding out wielding something that resembled a railway sleeper as a bat. The first ball he received was from Ryan and James hit it hard and flat for four straight back over the bowler's head. It thundered first bounce into the sight screen leaving a small cricket ball sized hole.

"Bloody hell," I said quietly so no-one else could hear.

"Nice shot!" Stuart called out and clapped a little too slowly for it to sound genuine.

James took a step down the wicket to the next ball, intent on hitting it further and harder but the young boy saw him coming and dug it in short and the ball hit James on the glove.

"That's it, Ryan," shouted Stuart. "Show him who's boss. Stick it up his nose."

James nearly took Ryan's head off with the last ball of the over as the bowler put up his hands in front of his face, more in self defence rather than a genuine attempt to catch it.

"Nearly had him there, Ryan. Better luck next time," said Stuart as we changed ends.

"Let's keep it friendly," Roger said quietly to Stuart as he passed by. "Remember, it's not a league game."

"Tell that to the batsman," said Stuart. "I mean, how old is your boy, sixteen?"

"Seventeen."

"And about 150 pounds dripping wet. He should pick on someone his own size."

"In case you haven't noticed we don't have anyone his size." Roger said.

"Skipper makes a good point," I said to Stuart but he ignored me.

"Keep going, kid. You're doing great," Stuart shouted to Ryan as the teenager jogged down to fine leg.

"Don't run, Ryan. Save it for your next over."

Roger took some punishment from James in the next over and split the webbing in his bowling hand trying to take a return catch from the last ball. He told Charles he was heading to the pavilion in search of the first aid kit.

"Take over for me, will you, Ben?" Roger said to me, clearly in a good deal of pain.

"Me? I've never captained a side in my life."

"I shan't be long. And you might be able to keep your friend from ending up in hospital if you can shut him up. That James character has quite the reputation."

"As a lover not a fighter?" I asked.

"No, quite the opposite," Roger said, trying to stem the flow of blood with a handkerchief. He walked off towards the pavilion to polite but somewhat nervous applause from his team.

Next over Stuart continued to encourage Ryan in a manner more or less appropriate to a friendly game of cricket from his position at a deepish mid off, positioned there in case James mishit one. James took a quick single off the last ball of the over to Stuart who hurled the ball just wide of the stumps hitting James a painful blow on the forearm as he ran his bat in. Stuart had a pretty strong arm and I saw James grimace with pain.

"Sorry, batsman," Stuart said, barely trying to fake sincerity. He put his arm around my shoulder at the change of ends.

"Give me one over at this bastard," he said to me under his breath. I looked over toward the pavilion but there was no sign of Roger returning to the field.

"Okay, one over," I said. "If you'll promise to keep your trap shut."

"Cross my heart." he said.

"And hope to die?" I asked.

Stuart took the ball from my hand.

"What field do you want?" I asked.

"What do you think?" It was very much a rhetorical question. He posted two men behind square for the hook and moved Ryan round in front of square.

"The kid can move. Let's hope he can catch," Stuart said to me out the corner of his mouth.

"I don't know who you're trying to fool," I said. "Your plan is not what I'd call subtle."

Stuart's over was not a raging success. His slingy action sends the ball down at a decent pace for our standard of cricket but a series of short balls and one attempted yorker all went for runs. Most of them to the boundary and all off James bat. He ran three off the last ball to keep the bowling.

Stuart took his cap back from the umpire and spoke to me in passing.

"Okay, two overs. Give me two overs."

Some of our team seemed to be finding this display of male machismo faintly amusing, especially as James treated Ryan's next over with exaggerated respect and a series of dead bat defensive shots. He took a single off the last ball so with Roger still off the field I reluctantly tossed the ball to Stuart.

Stuart winked at me and turned his cap back to front baseball style instead of handing it to the umpire. Charles raised an eyebrow as if to say 'must you, Stuart? Really?' and sighed audibly when Stuart announced he was going to bowl round the wicket. I was surprised Charles hadn't stepped in to calm things down but he seemed to be enjoying the drama and disappointed by Stuart's antics in equal measure.

Stuart's first ball duly sailed high over midwicket off James' bat, just missing Faith and her kids who had obviously just arrived. Stuart called out to her.

"Hello, Faith. Watch out for the artillery."

Stuart's next ball was an effort ball, short and outside of the off stump and James should have cut it for four but, perhaps incensed by Stuart's remark he tried another pull shot which came off the top edge and Ryan moved quickly around and caught the ball high above his head a yard inside the rope.

Most of our players went over to congratulate the fielder but I was watching Stuart who was breathing hard with his hands on his knees and a huge grin on his face.

James slowly walked off to the applause of his team mates in the pavilion. Nobody knew where the key to the score box was kept so how many runs he'd scored was for now a mystery. I was just glad to see the back of him, given the way in which he had scored them.

"Inspired piece of captaincy, Ben," Charles said.

"Thanks, but it was all Stuart's plan," I said, loud enough I hoped for it to register with James. There was a loud crash of bat on dressing room wall as he left the field of play.

After Roger returned to take over, things got back to some sort of normality after a fashion. The rest of London Theatre's batsmen played sensibly and they scored close to two hundred before declaring at tea time.

The strawberry tart was indeed delicious though I wasn't really very hungry. Stuart tucked into the sandwiches two at a time. I noticed Roger talking to Ryan for a few minutes before he came over to us. "Batting three and four, okay, fellas?" he said to us with a nod. It didn't really sound like a question. "My boy fancies opening. Thinks there might be a scout watching that he wants to impress."

"Thanks, skip," said Stuart. We won't let you down."

"What's with the 'we', White Man?" I said after Roger had gone.

"Relax, Kemosabe."

"Have you noticed, James is nowhere to be seen?"

"Probably hiding in the toilets," said Stuart

"Probably sharpening his spikes," I said.

James as it turned out was sharing a teatime picnic with his family and came straight out onto the field from where they sat on the boundary edge without going back to the pavilion.

Predictably he took the new ball from one end but I was glad to see that he was running in off just a half dozen paces. You could see he had a strong action in his delivery side but he looked to be bowling very much within himself.

Ryan opened the batting and looked pretty good doing it. The other opener's name I had already forgotten and he seemed nervous facing James. The bowler at the other end didn't look like anything to be concerned about.

Ryan hit a nice four off the back foot to get off the mark in James' second over and I was heartened to see James pause at the end of his follow through and applaud the batsman along with several other fielders though I did notice they didn't clap before James started putting his hands together.

"Nice shot, son," Roger said.

"He can really play, your lad," I said.

"Thanks," said Roger. "I'm taking down for a trial at Hampshire next week."

"He'll do well, I'm sure. You know, Roger…"

I was about to politely suggest that he might move me down the batting order when Ryan's partner managed to run himself out in what looked like an attempt to avoid facing James, who was the fielder in question and showed himself to have an arm like a slingshot.

"Don't take any liberties on his throw, will you, Ben. Good luck."

"Cry havoc and let slip the dogs of war!" was, I thought, less than helpful parting advice from Stuart, considering the sticky end Mark Antony came to shortly after that particular call to arms.

The bat seemed very alien in my hands as I walked out and took my guard. I took a deep breath and patted down the pitch for no good reason other than to delay the inevitable. Ryan tapped gloves with me and said something encouraging like "he's not that quick. Just watch the ball and play yourself in". I wasn't really listening to be honest.

It was comforting to see Charles up the other end as umpire. Less comforting to see the towering figure of James with ball in hand a few paces behind him. I took my guard on middle and leg and tried to remember how I used to stand. I plunged forward to

James' first ball, sticking to my default setting of forward defence as if playing from memory only to find the ball thudding into my bottom glove and trapping my hand against the bat handle. I did a passable imitation of someone trying to start a chainsaw as I withdrew my hand off the bat a crucial fraction of a second too late. My hand was numb with pain.

"Great," I thought. "I couldn't play the bastard with two hands on the bat."

I walked down the wicket to pat down where I thought the ball had pitched but knew that the pitch wasn't to blame. I was really only playing for time. Ryan met me mid pitch.

"How's your hand? Bowls a heavy ball, doesn't he."

"Perhaps they've got a lighter one he can use."

"No, I meant-"

"I know what you meant. I was joking."

"Try moving back and across. Get your feet moving. Play him off the back foot if you can."

"That's probably good advice."

The next two balls I tried to follow Ryan's advice but didn't get close to laying bat on ball. I was at least relieved to have some respite from ball on Ben. I guessed that both balls had moved away from me in the air or off the pitch but truth be told it was too fast for me to see it. The ball was already past me as I tried to move into line to play a shot. Each time it hit the keeper's gloves with an intimidating thwack. Anticipating that James' next delivery might move the other way did not help me one bit. It hit me on the inside of my back thigh and I heard a concerted appeal for lbw which at least drowned out my involuntary whimper of pain.

"Not out," said Charles.

""Too high, umpire?" I heard James ask.

"Just a little. Going over the top, I thought."

The next ball hit me flush on the foot and somehow failed to hit the stumps on its way past. Another appeal, louder this time.

"Please give me out, Charles," I thought. "Please put your finger up."

"Not out," said Charles. "Missing leg."

"Didn't miss mine," I muttered.

Someone in the slips behind me laughed though whether he was laughing with me or at me I couldn't say. I took guard again, opening my stance in the hope of avoiding another blow on my foot. I was also hoping my attempt at gallows humour might bring some sympathy from James. I was mistaken. I heard James grunt from the extra effort he put into his delivery stride for the last ball of the over but I never saw it. It hit me flush on the side of the helmet as I ducked into the path of the ball. Clearly the ball hadn't been as short as I thought it was.

"Sorry, batsman," I heard from James, my tormentor, a few yards distant at the end of his follow through. His apology sounded less than sincere. "It wasn't that short."

"No, just short enough," I muttered as I got back to my feet.

I wanted to add the words 'you bastard' but managed to stop myself from questioning the legitimacy of the circumstances surrounding his birth.

"Try keeping your eye on the ball," James said. It sounded more like sarcasm than any attempt to give helpful advice.

"Are you alright, Ben?" It was Charles' welcome and avuncular interruption.

"Is that you, mother?" I said.

"How many fingers am I holding up?" Charles said, smiling while holding up his little finger.

"Just the one and not the one I was hoping for. I take it that wasn't hitting the stumps either."

"Just going over the top, I thought," Charles said.

"Sounds close enough for me," I said.

"Didn't have the heart to give it out," Charles said.

"Not when you were shaping up so well."

"Do you want to know which finger I'd like to give you, Charles?"

"Don't be vulgar. Shall we get on with the game, gentlemen?"

Charles give me a pat on the back. It was little comfort to my foot or ears which were still ringing from the blow on the helmet.

"Think you'd better take a breather," I heard their captain say.

"I couldn't agree more," I said.

"I'm talking to my bowler."

"Thanks for seeing him off, Ben. I'll take it from here. Go and have a seat in the shade. No disgrace in retiring hurt."

It was Stuart's voice coming from somewhere behind me. I turned a little unsteadily to see Stuart, bat under one arm, approaching the batting crease. He was pulling on his batting gloves for which, dear Lord, I was truly grateful. I limped off unsteadily towards the pavilion.

"Are you okay, Ben?" Faith called out from where she was standing.

"I'll live."

Polite applause from my team mates greeted my return to the pavilion and I jokingly raised my bat as if I'd scored a hundred, something I had never in my cricketing life achieved. I was fairly certain in that moment that I never would. I had retired hurt in more ways than one.

I saw in the mirror on the wall that I had a small cut on the side of my face but nothing life threatening. I sat down and slowly took my kit off, knowing that I was not going to resume my innings under any circumstances, even if the captain's hand on my shoulder smote. One smote a day was quite enough and as far as I was concerned I'd played my last game of cricket.

I could hear applause and and cries of "shot" from my team mates. When I came back outside it was clear that Ryan with some style and panache and Stuart with a little more joyous and reckless abandon had turned the tide our way and were putting together the beginnings of a promising partnership. They began to take their toll of the less threatening bowlers their skipper had called on in the hope of making it a game of it.

James twice went over to their captain to suggest or more likely demand that he bowl the next over but the captain shook his head each time. The conversation got a little more animated the third time before James took the ball forcibly from the skipper's hand and gave his cap and sweater to Charles.

"Change of bowler. Right arm over, batsman."

"Thank you, Charles," said Stuart.

Stuart elaborately marked out a fresh guard making the bowler wait an unnecessarily long time. He thrashed James' loosener backward of point. The next ball was short and Stuart pulled it for four, swivelling on his back foot, Caribbean style. James went back to his mark. Once there he picked the white disc and returned to the crease before marking out a new and much longer run up. I counted thirty-nine steps.

He thundered in off this longer run and put Stuart on his backside with a short delivery that reared up and hit the peak of Stuart's cap as he dropped to the floor in a heap. Stuart picked up his cap and dusted it off before replacing it on his head. James glared at him and shared a few choice words. Stuart raised his cap by way of response as if he was Derek Randall facing Dennis Lillee in their famous confrontation in the Centenary Test.

"No, Stuart, don't do that." I heard Roger say. "I don't think that's wise."

"He can't help himself, " I said. "It's in his nature."

"It'll be in his ear if he's not careful."

"Round the wicket, umpire," James said without ever taking his eyes off Stuart.

Charles shared a few words with James as he walked past which seemed to incense him further if that were possible. Ryan was close enough at the non striker's end to overhear the exchange of views. He looked over towards his father in the pavilion as if wanting his advice. All this time Stuart was leaning on his bat handle as if he didn't have a care in the world.

"Do you think he'll take him off for intimidatory bowling?" I asked.

"Not so long as Stuart doesn't look intimidated," Roger said.

"That's what I'm afraid of."

"Round the wicket, batsman," Charles said.

Stuart looked round the field and took a long lingering look in the direction of square leg as if to anticipate his next shot which I thought was an act of stupidity beyond words.

The next ball was fast and short as everyone including Stuart knew it would be and somehow he hooked it almost off the end of his nose. It flew off the top edge of his bat over backward square leg. I spotted Faith gathering up her things and walking with her kids towards the car park. Apparently she'd seen enough. Nobody else moved. A 'breathless hush' indeed.

Charles exchanged more words with James and this time he beckoned their captain over who said nothing to Charles but merely nodded in agreement and had a word with James before returning to his position at mid off. James went back to his mark. Another bumper followed which Stuart made to hook again but missed before sitting down in a mess of arms and legs and stayed like that as if slightly surprised to find his head still attached to his shoulders.

Charles walked up to the stumps and removed the bails before speaking in a calm, clear baritone voice. "And that, gentlemen, concludes the play for the day."

I wondered if he'd been aware of the possible theatrical play on words and thought, knowing Charles, that he probably had. James kicked at the ground in impotent rage, right in the middle of the pitch. Stuart collected his limbs together and tucked his bat under his arm. He shook hands with the opposing skipper who gave him a pat on the shoulder as if to say well played. Still mid-pitch, James stopped Stuart with a few private words. He was obviously not enquiring after Stuart's well-being. Stuart said nothing by way of reply which looked like a very smart move and James headed straight from the field towards the car park. Some of our team clapped Stuart on the back or shook his hand but it was a strangely muted atmosphere while everyone came to terms with the abandonment of the game. Stuart went into our team's changing room and sat down. I followed him in and sat beside him.

"What did he say to you?" I asked.

"He said 'stay the fuck away from my wife'."

Chapter Forty-Two

"*The Play's the Thing...*"

"...wherein I'll catch the conscience of the King."
It was safe to assume that James knew nothing of
Hamlet's wheeze to put on a play to confirm his
uncle's guilt. But the only reason for a jealous
husband to come to our show three nights in a row
was presumably to see some evidence of impropriety
on his wife's part.

And on each of these three nights I could see that
there were subtle differences in Faith and Stuart's
performances which increased the onstage friction in
some places and dampened down the chemistry in
others. The performance was significantly different in
tone. And on each night Faith gathered her things
quickly and left with her husband after the show,
leaving Stuart and I in the dressing room with an
uncomfortable silence between us.

Under normal circumstances the director might have
had a word with the cast to pull things back to how
they had been in rehearsal. The play was by no means
a light comedy but it had been joy to perform. It
seemed like now the joy had gone from the

performance. On the third such night I couldn't stand it any longer.

"Stuart, James doesn't have any reason to keep coming here, does he?"

"Apart from his new found love of the theatre you mean?"

"Yes."

"No, Ben there's not."

"No reason for him to be jealous?"

"Of what?"

"You and Faith. There's nothing going on, right?"

"No, Ben, there's nothing going on. And if there were, what the hell would it have to do with you?"

"So why has James taken to haunting the theatre all of a sudden?"

"Because he's a fucking psycho or hadn't you noticed?"

"Okay, I just wanted to-"

"Just drop it, Ben. There's nothing going on between me and Faith. Okay?"

Chapter Forty-Three
Play False

On the fourth night of Othello's stalking of
Desdemona, the Moor of Venice couldn't get into the
auditorium. Sometimes a theatre will say it's sold out
but tickets get returned at the last minute. On this
night there wasn't a seat to be had. I could hear James
arguing with the usher and offering her money if he
could have her seat. To give her credit she stood up to
him remarkably well from what I could hear and
calmly explained that she didn't have a seat and
would be standing inside the door for the whole
performance. And no, he couldn't stand next to her.
There were fire regulations to be adhered to. I heard
that the manager of the pub who owned the venue had
to be called and James was threatened with an
encounter with the bouncer if he didn't leave.
Not what you'd call a great start to the evening.
Backstage I could see Faith biting her lip and fighting
back the tears. Stuart gave her a hug and said a few
comforting words and she nodded in agreement but
Stuart was right. It looked like Faith just had the
misfortune to be married to a six foot four guy with
massive anger and jealousy issues.
I couldn't help wondering at that moment why such a
nice, loveable, gentle woman, how a perfectly nice, I
mean, *perfectly* nice woman could fall for a bastard

like that. I caught myself thinking "God, it's just like the play. Judy falls for Stuart when there's a perfectly nice guy like Dai right in front of her…"

A guy just like me. Except that wasn't true. Because I was jealous too. I wanted to be the guy holding her, comforting her. Not Stuart. Even if there was nothing else going on, I wanted to be that guy.

I found myself sitting alone in my flat at night after the show wondering if I'd missed something in the play. Maybe it wasn't as simple as a hard luck story about the nice guy getting the girl in the end before his best friend, her husband, kills him in a fit of jealousy. Maybe Dai wasn't such a nice guy after all. Maybe there was something rather sad and creepy about a guy hanging out around his best friend's family, secretly hoping that the marriage would fail. Stuart's character in the play was a complete player, a cheating bastard, but did that make it alright to want to sleep with someone else's wife?

That didn't make Dai a good friend. That made him a false friend.

Chapter Forty-Four

Play Down

What with the prospect of stalkers, both real and perhaps imaginary in the audience, and feeling now that I might have written the play differently, the joy had gone. In spite of the fact that we were still playing to packed houses, I didn't look forward to coming in to the theatre to do the play. So I was secretly quite relieved when Fiona picked me up from home to give me a lift into town for the final performance so that I could have a few drinks afterwards without having to drive home.

"You're very quiet, this evening," she said in the car. "Cat got your tongue?" she asked.

"The cat can keep it for a while. I think I've had my fill of talking. Sorry, it's just been a strange few weeks."

"No chance of getting back together with Jo? She seemed to make you happy for a while."

"No, she's polishing some other cricketer's balls now."

"If that's some sort of sporting euphemism, I'm not familiar with it."

"It's not a euphemism."

"Cheer up. The play's a hit. You're the hot, new young writer in town so I hear."

"Not feeling so young. Or hot. But someone did send me an email about possibly taking the play on tour."

"That's good, isn't it?"

"I guess. We'd have to re-cast though. Faith's got her kids so she can't tour and I'm tired of doing some stupid Welsh accent. No, that's not true. The silly accent is the only thing that's got me through the last few nights. And I haven't had a chance to ask Stuart yet. So…"

"I think you need to give yourself a bit more credit. It's a really good play, Ben."

"So everyone keeps telling me. Thanks."

With ten minutes to go before the show I suddenly noticed that something about Faith's costume looked different.

"You're wearing a scarf…"

Faith touched the silk scarf round her neck reflexively.

"I've got some kind of rash. It's from a new necklace I've got."

"Okay, sorry. I just wondered why…"

"It's just a rash, Ben. Some kind of allergic reaction." Stuart interrupted. "Ben, it's nearly time for 'beginners'. Let's go."

"Yeah, once more unto the breach, folks. See you out there, Faith."

The show seemed to go by in a flash and there was no sign of James or hooded sweatshirts. For the curtain call, Faith was in the middle between me and Stuart as usual. She gave my hand a noticeable squeeze on our third bow which she'd never done before. I glanced across at her and saw Stuart was likewise looking back so I guess she'd squeezed both our hands. Maybe she's still in character, I thought.

I found my face reddening with embarrassment when I saw Fiona stepping onto the stage with a huge bouquet of flowers. I stared at her as if to say, "don't you dare give those to me."

She leaned forward and whispered in my ear.

"They're not for you, you idiot," before handing them to Faith.

"Who were the flowers from?" I asked as we walked back to the dressing room. "Do you have a secret admirer?"

"No, just a husband."

"Oh God, what did he do wrong now?" I asked.

Faith went to put the flowers in a jug of water but not before I saw her brushing away a tear.

"Don't tell me I'm allergic to flowers now as well," she said, wiping her eyes with a tissue.

"See you downstairs in the pub, Ben," said Stuart.

Quite a few friends and acquaintances had managed to get tickets for the last show and although we hadn't planned a last night party, I could see straight away that I was likely to be in the pub till closing time.

There was even some applause when I came into the bar which was faintly embarrassing. I've never even enjoyed the applause at curtain calls very much.

"Did you get my text about Faith's flowers?" asked Fiona.

"No, what did it say? I gather they were from her ogre of a husband." I reached my hand into an empty pocket. "Hang on to my pint, will you? I must have left my phone in the dressing room."

I passed Jo and Paul on my way to the door.

"Is the dressing room still open?" I asked Jo. "I forgot my mobile."

"I've just locked it. I'll go with you. Don't want to lose the keys on the last night."

We could still hear the music from the pub as Jo unlocked the door at the top of the stairs. I picked up my phone from where I'd left it. As I turned to leave I saw movement and a reflection in one of the mirrors. Stuart and Faith were slow dancing in the dark corridor that led from the far side of the dressing room to the toilet.

I turned and rejoined Jo, still standing outside the door. She closed it quietly and locked it.

"It's okay," she said

"No, it's not. It's a long fucking way from okay."

And I started to cry. Jo reached out to me and held me tight.

"No," she said. "I meant... They can get out okay. They've got their own key."

Chapter Forty-Five
Play Over

I sat down on the stairs between the dressing room and the pub below.

"I don't know why I'm crying. It's got nothing to do with me," I said, though I wondered who I was trying to convince.

"No, Ben. It doesn't. It doesn't have anything to do with you."

"How long has this been going on?"

"Not long. But it's been a long time coming. James attacked her last night. She's moved in to her mum's with the kids… Come on, let's go back down. You look like you could do with a drink."

"Think I'd rather just slip off quietly and go home."

"Ben, I know you've had this thing for Faith for like forever, but it's time you got over that and in a hurry. Faith and Stuart need you to act like a friend not like some jealous teenager. So get down into that bar and stop feeling sorry for yourself. Man up!"

I did my best to man up for about forty-five minutes. Faith and Stuart came down together but didn't stay long. After they'd left I quietly brought Fiona up to speed with the situation and she took pity on me and drove me home.

Chapter Forty-Six
Play Off

There's generally a strange hiatus of a few days, sometimes longer, after a play closes. It's a bit like peace breaking out after the period of dramatic conflict. You no longer have your daily routine of waking up late, nap in the afternoon, and late night supper and a drink after the show.

This period of unsettled calm was all the stranger in that I was single again and didn't feel I could call Stuart up. I'd sent Faith a text the next day to say how sorry I was for what she was going through. I didn't let on that I knew anything about her and Stuart. I guess I hoped that somehow my silence might imply they had my good wishes.

So it came as something of a relief when Stuart and I had to drive up to Scotland a couple of weeks later. Our old schoolfriend Johnny had got in touch to say that he and his wife were flying over from Australia and had booked into Gleneagles Hotel for three nights with their newly married daughter and her husband. They were going to have a small ceremony to re-celebrate the wedding because his father, a widower, had not been well enough to make the long flight to Australia.

We'd taken Stuart's car because I remained unconvinced of the Alfa's reliability in the wet and it's nearly impossible to fit two bags in it, let alone two sets of golf clubs.

The long drive north gave Stuart and I the chance to catch up and I found it surprisingly easy to wish him and Faith the best of luck. About forty miles south of Gleneagles I told Stuart my father's story about how the elderly gent who owned Gleneagles House used to get thoroughly irate when answering phone calls meant for the nearby hotel. His usual riposte was "I think you are trying to reach the hostelry down the road."

There had been no room at that particular inn for a late booking so Stuart and I were staying at the ghastly mock Tudor hotel in Blackford, the village with the apocalyptic weather where I had once lived. And yes, it started to rain as we drove into the village. We weren't invited to the family dinner at Gleneagles so I took Stuart out for a pint and a steak dinner at the little pub across the road from my old house.

It was under new management. The steaks weren't quite as good as I remembered them and I was quietly relieved not to see a list of names comprising a 'dead pool' on the wall behind the bar or the surly drunk who had always been one of the semi-permanent fixtures and fittings.

Next morning the sun broke through the clouds as we left the village and made the short drive north on the A9 to the hotel. It was nice to see Johnny again after so long, though his father, Les, had aged a good deal and said categorically that he would be a spectator and watch our game from the comfort of a golf cart. I protested that he should at least have a sneaky putt or two if nobody was watching. After witnessing my appalling form on the greens he started taking my putts for me which kept me vaguely in touch with the rest in terms of score. Stuart played well and behaved better than usual because Les was there. Johnny played a steady game. His new son-in-law, Stephen, was clearly a class above us and I got the impression he was holding back on the tee so as not to embarrass the rest of us, who were all a bunch of hackers by comparison.

I was relieved to spend more time on the fairway than usual rather than holding everyone up looking for my mishit balls in the rough, though this also meant that Stuart only found one golf ball on his way round.

"I think that's the same ball Tiger Woods plays," he said as he dropped it into the pocket of his golf trousers whose colour and design were unusually muted.

All in all we had a pretty pleasant time of it. We'd had to take quite an early tee time so Johnny and I trooped off to try a bit of clay pigeon shooting. Stuart and Stephen went back to the hotel with Les, who said he was a little tired and wanted to have a lie down before lunch.

We'd arrived a little early for our appointment at the shooting range so there would be a short delay before we could get kitted up. The shooting coach explained he was just finishing up with an earlier booking and apologised that his colleague had had some car trouble and hadn't arrived for work yet.

"Doesn't drive an Alfa Romeo, does he?"

"Yes, as a matter of fact he does. How did you know?"

"Lucky guess."

We said not to worry as we were waiting for a couple of friends. I was telling Johnny about our recent adventures on the cricket field. I had just got to the point where Stuart was about to take guard against James off his long run up when I heard a familiar voice behind me.

"Hello, Benjamin."

I turned around to see someone getting out of another golf cart. It was a moment before I realised it was my brother. He'd put on an enormous amount of weight since I'd seen him last and was wearing a golf cap and a hooded sweat shirt, putting his face in shadow at first. It was only after he pulled the hood down and took off a pair aviator sunglasses that I realised who it was.

"Don't recognise your own brother?" he asked. It wasn't a friendly question.

"No, you look... How are you?"

"I saw the announcement of your pal's wedding ceremony in the paper and put two and two together. I've been following you round the golf course, waiting for my chance."

"Your chance for what? To speak to me?"

By way of reply he reached into the golf bag in the back of his golf cart. They say that witnesses in a bank robbery often struggle to give an accurate description of the bank robber but can give the police a very accurate description of the gun he was holding. My brother, Ken, was holding what looked like a vintage, but still lethal looking, shotgun. For some strange reason the name Purdey came into my head as a make of shotgun but this hardly seemed to be an appropriate time to learn about firearms except that I now knew that time seems to slow down when someone is pointing one at you.

"Get out of that golf cart," he said. "And tell your friend to stay where he is."

I did as I was told and glanced over to the shooting range guy who was holding a shotgun himself but was talking to some other guests a good forty yards away. He had his back to us and was going to be no help at all in the immediate future. Assuming I had anything longer than an immediate future. My brother pulled back on the twin hammers to cock both barrels. 'So this is it. This is how I'm going to die,' I thought. 'Didn't even get close to my next birthday.'

My eyes continued to focus on the gun. I never saw Stuart and Stephen approaching in their electric golf cart. And my brother, Ken, never saw the Nike One Platinum Gold golf ball that Stuart threw at him. The ball hit my brother a considerable blow on the temple and he collapsed in stages, first to his knees and then forward onto his stomach.

"Fore!" shouted Stuart.

There was a terrible ringing sound in my ears and smoke coming from one of the barrels of the shotgun but it was a few seconds before I realised I'd been shot. Johnny ran forward to pick up the shotgun. He was seemingly unhurt.

I've know idea what the spread of pellets is like from a shotgun at close range but I was grateful to see that the back of our golf cart seemed to have taken most of the blast. I looked down to see specks of blood were starting to leech through my right trouser leg.

I was even more relieved to see the other member of the Alfa Romeo owners' club arrive by electric cart with another guest who was quite literally "riding shotgun". I don't know if he'd had training in dealing with an incident like this but he immediately took charge. He secured my still groggy brother's wrists with a pair of cable ties and took charge of my brother's discharged shotgun. He removed the spent shells just to make sure.

The police arrived in a remarkably short time to take my brother away just as he was regaining consciousness. One of police officers sounded like he'd had dealings with Ken before which made me wonder what else my brother had been up to since I'd seen him last.

The wedding ceremony went ahead as scheduled though Stuart and I were missing from proceedings. Stephen and Johnny had decided it best to conceal what had just taken place until at least later in the day. It was almost dinner time when Stuart and I returned from the emergency room in nearby Perth to join the others for an early supper. The hotel had suddenly found a suite of rooms available for Stuart and I which they gave to us at what I guessed was a considerable discount for as long as we wanted while I recovered.

What with the painkillers and a couple of glasses of wine at dinner, I was pretty exhausted and very grateful for the sanctuary of my bedroom and a relatively peaceful night's sleep thanks to one of Fiona's sleeping tablets I'd kept in my wallet for emergencies.

A near death experience at the hands of a family member seemed to qualify as an emergency.

Chapter Forty-Seven

Playing for Time

The next morning I woke up with a very sore leg I couldn't put much weight on. I didn't much enjoy being pushed around in a wheel chair and I could see that Stuart was starting to get antsy after a day and a half of playing nurse maid. I didn't appreciate him texting while he was "driving" either, but I could see he was missing Faith and wanted to get back down south. So, after I found I could hobble around with just a walking stick on the third day, I released him from his duties as hospital orderly and he left that same afternoon.

My credit still seemed good with the hotel and perhaps because they wanted to avoid any bad publicity or because I had become a minor celebrity with the staff I could not say enough about their kindness. They were always offering me complimentary massages and the like. Perhaps that's just how you get treated if you have a suite of rooms at a swanky hotel, I don't know.

With Stuart and the wedding party gone I began to feel a little bored and was looking up train times back to London when the phone in my room rang on the fifth morning. I'd made enquiries at the front desk earlier about how I could amuse myself during my stay. Golf and shooting were clearly out of the question as far as I was concerned. Falconry didn't excite me as I've never been especially fond of birds unless they were on my dinner plate.

The receptionist said she was passing the phone over to the head of the equestrian centre who informed me they'd had a cancellation for a carriage driving lesson and would I like to give it a try. I wasn't all that keen and protested that I hadn't brought my top hat and tails but she was pretty persuasive that they would be able to hoist me into the driver's seat. I said I would think about it for ten minutes then call them back. What eventually sealed the deal was the front page of their website which bore the following quotation:

"No hour of life is wasted that is spent in the saddle" (Winston Churchill).

Thinking if it's good enough for Churchill... And also having nothing much better to do with my time, I agreed to meet the manager of the equestrian centre in half an hour downstairs in the lobby.

She drove me by golf buggy to the stables. I found myself thinking about the scene in *When Harry Met Sally* when they're out Christmas shopping and Billy Crystal picks up the microphone of a karaoke machine and starts singing the song from the musical *Oklahoma* about going for a carriage ride with your best gal. And I found myself still quietly singing as I went into the stable block with the smell of fresh straw in my nostrils.

"Chicks and ducks and geese better scurry,
When I take you out in the Surrey,

*When I take you out in the Surrey with the fringe on
top.
Watch that fringe and see how it flutters
When I drive them high steppin' strutters
Nosy folks'll peek through their shutters and their
eyes will pop..."*

What makes Harry's eyes go pop and stops him mid-
verse is the sight of his ex-wife with her new man
coming towards them in the store. What stopped me
singing was the sight of a strangely familiar face
looking up from behind the hindquarters of a horse as
she pulled a brush through the tuft of hair at the back
of its leg.

"Fetlocks," I said because 'fuck me' might have
seemed rude by way of a greeting.

"*Bonjour, Ben...*"

"Marie...?"

"How are you? How's your leg?"

"It's fine. It's sore... It's okay. You can speak English
now."

"Yes, I read the newspaper every morning to improve
my vocabulary. That's how I found out about you and
you're brother and... he might have killed you."

"It was predictable. Apparently."

"Sorry, I don't understand."

"It was predictable... apparently that something like
that might happen. Someone told me that something
like that... Never mind. I'll explain later. It's a long
story... Your English is very good."

"I think I have too strong an accent still."

"No, I like it… it sounds cute."

"Is that good? I thought that 'cute' is for puppies, no?"

"It's a very nice accent. God, it's great to see you…"

And we rode off together on a horse drawn carriage. Not into the sunset as is traditional at this point in a story but into the bright high noon sunshine. Maybe not quite Gary Cooper and Grace Kelly but I imagined we looked like a cute couple. Even cuter than a couple of puppies. I couldn't help my heart filling with song once more after our first kiss since our one night together in France.

And, yes, I did actually sing on our way back in our Surrey with no fringe on top.

"Oh what a beautiful morning,

Oh what a beautiful day.

I've got a wonderful feeling

Everything's going my way."

What can I say? It was a very long, very lovely kiss. It turns out a carriage ride with your best gal is a very romantic way to travel and I thoroughly recommend you try it some day.

And that's about all, folks…

I hope you didn't skip to the end of the story like Billy Crystal and that this ending came to you as a big and beautiful surprise as it did to me. Near death and then… this.

I'm thinking about what next while writing this in the small, one bedroom flat which Marie rents in

Auchterarder, just to the north of Gleneagles. My leg's nearly better. We're a few miles away from my new four legged friends and it's not quite such a romantic setting as our first night together, Marie's previous apartment in the loft above the horses' stables in the French Alps where she worked in the summer. But sometimes when I lie awake at night I can remember the sound of them whinnying or stamping their hooves. And sometimes in my dreams I think I hear them still.

Speaking of romance Stuart and Faith are still together. It turns out he loves being a stay at home dad which is just as well because Faith's got herself a significant role in what they hope will be the next big thing on Netflix. They start shooting in a couple of months somewhere in Poland apparently. So Stuart's going to sublet his flat in London and they're going to rent a place in Warsaw for the four of them. Stuart's going to home school the kids and promises to steer clear of lessons in Lifemanship. As for Fiona, she's dating the divorced father of one of her dance pupils. Apparently he's very nice and drives a really sensible car with plenty of legroom which doesn't leak when it rains.

And Jo still thinks Paul is gorgeous.

As for me and the whole life and death thing, predictions of impending doom and so forth… Has it already happened or is it still to happen? Was my destiny changed by Stuart's right arm and a well aimed golf ball? My brother's day in court and also my next birthday are both coming up so I guess I'll find out soon enough. And maybe, if I can, I'll let you know.

You've maybe heard the joke about the man who falls off the roof of a skyscraper. Maybe you're of a darker frame of mind than I am right now and think I'm that guy. Who can every really know what the future holds? Maybe I'm like that guy and maybe I'm not. One thing I can say for certain is that for the first time since my last birthday I actually do feel like I've won the lottery. And so all I can really say for now is this. I don't know whether I'm falling or flying but...so far so good.

THE END

Author's Note: I regret to say that winning the lottery was not one of the bits that were true.

If you enjoyed this book please take a moment to leave a review on Amazon and share with your friends on social media.

Thank you.

Printed in Great Britain
by Amazon